SECRETS

of a

FANGIRL

SECRETS of a FANGIRL

ERIN DIONNE

SCHOLASTIC INC.

ISBN 978-1-338-57654-2

10 9 8 7 6 5 4 3 2 1   19 20 21 22 23

Printed in the U.S.A.   40
First printing 2019
Book design by Maeve Norton

FOR CHARLOTTE POE,
WHO IS FIERCELY HERSELF

RULES & CONS

1

"Sarah Anne! Look!"

For the hundredth time, Dad grabs my arm and points. This time, it's a life-sized Chewbacca with his weapon-thing.

"Yup. Cool," I say, hoping my flat voice gives him the clue that I'm done goggling at the assorted aliens, superheroes, monsters, and zombies. I keep my eyes on the signs pointing us to Hall C, where we'll find the Nightshade panel, and hope that my stomach settles by the time we get there.

Entering the MK Nightshade trivia contest seemed like a good idea at eleven p.m. on a random Tuesday in February. I was deep into my whatever-number reread of *A Glut of Ghosts* and had gone online looking for info about the release date of the movie. It wouldn't be out until May, but the blinking banner on the movie page read: "MK Nightshade Ultimate Trivia Contest!!! Fantastic Fans Will Win Prizes!!" The questions were so easy. I thought I'd win a T-shirt, not an invitation to be on a panel at FanCon.

Someone jumps in front of me, blue cape swirling. I almost crash into him, but he doesn't even glance in my direction.

"You'll never terrorize Gotham City again!" Old-school Batman points a gloved hand at The Joker and The Riddler, who are strolling down the concourse on the other side of my dad. They all crack up.

"Dude, take our picture?" The Joker, in full makeup and the purple suit, hands his phone to my dad, who happily steps in. I step behind the nearest pole and rub my temples. My heart thuds in my chest and my stomach rolls like Sir Oakheart's boat in the storm in *A Sea of Serpents*.

I take a breath, hold it, and let it out, like my lacrosse coach, Ms. Vaughn, taught us to do when we're nervous.

I peek around the pole: Batman and the gang pose for another pic. Behind them, a group of girls around my age dressed in matching Vampire Skool T-shirts and black lipstick come toward us, snickering. I pull my head back, fast.

Uggghhhh. This whole scenario violates one of my major rules: Keep your Geek on the down low.

In elementary school, it was okay to wear character T-shirts and carry a *Star Wars* lunch box. But by the time I got to middle school, being so into a fandom was not cool anymore—sports and hair and clothes were.

At least, that's what's cool to my friends. Since I want to keep being friends with them, I stick to those guidelines. So far, I always have a party to go to and people to eat lunch with—unlike the kids who still carry those *Star Wars* lunch boxes.

Crossed arms over my chest, I wait for the girls to pass my hiding spot. Hopefully none of them go to Howard Hoffer Junior High with me — or sense the giant Nightshade-dork beacon that I feel is attached to me.

One of the girls spots me and cackles. What the . . . ?

"Oh. My. God. It's Princess Perfect! Great costume!" The others turn to me.

"That's hilarious!" says another.

I glance down: pink-and-purple sparkly tunic, charcoal leggings, and boots. My BFF, Roxy, told me pink and purple are totally in this season, and if she says it's in, that's what I wear.

Princess Perfect . . . ?

"My four-year-old sister loves that show," the third says. "All you need is her big bow and you'd nail it."

It clicks: Princess Perfect is a cartoon character on the Beanpole network. I want to climb a beanpole right out of here. Instead I give them a weak smile as they goth on their way.

"Sarah Anne —?" Dad's voice breaks through my thoughts. Batman and the villains are gone — presumably back to Gotham City — and Dad's turning in a slow circle looking for me.

"Sorry," I say, crossing the floor. "I wanted to check something out."

"We need to get you to the panel," he responds. "No more lingering."

"As if I'm the one who stopped to chat with the Justice League," I mutter under my breath.

Dad cocks an eyebrow at me but doesn't say anything. Instead, he takes a deep breath and pushes his glasses up on his nose. We follow the Hall C signs again. But two steps later his head swivels as he takes in the costumes and merch. We're in the *Star Wars* section.

Two kids dressed in Jedi robes stage a mock lightsaber battle.

"Jedi don't fight one another." This time it's Dad doing the muttering and me giving the side-eye.

Dad's a total *Star Wars* geek. He and Mom have been into it for years. Coming here is almost more of a treat for him than for me. Luckily I talked him out of wearing his VADER FOR PRESIDENT T-shirt, but had to compromise with his Boba Fett tee. At home this morning I thought his outfit was embarrassing. Now? He's fitting in better than I do, so there's that.

I kind of wanted to wear the MY OTHER HORSE IS A CHARIOT Sir Oakheart T-shirt that my sister, Penny, gave me for Christmas, but it definitely makes Roxy's "fashion don't" list. I only wear it to bed.

A girl dressed as some alien creature strolls by, trailing tentacles from a mess of long dreadlocks. A couple in solid Lucius and Narcissa Malfoy costumes stop for a photo with an okay-looking Voldemort. Bunches of zombies, some with really good makeup, others looking like Halloween costumes gone wrong, stagger past.

What am I *doing* here?

I mean, I love MK Nightshade and his world and all, but this is . . . a bit much.

Dad keeps pointing and walking slower and I just want to get this over with.

And then there it is: a huge — I mean *huge* — replica of Castle Crepacuore, complete with the Forsaken Turret where Lady Althena was held captive for sixty-five nights in *A Mausoleum of Monsters.*

I freeze.

"Cool, huh?" Dad says, nudging me. I just nod. He gives my arm another nudge and we move closer to the castle. It has to be thirty feet tall! Maybe bigger. The ceilings in the convention hall are super high, but still. It's *tall.*

When we get through the crowd at the base of the castle, I read the banner hanging across a table near the gate: THE MK NIGHT-SHADE X-PERIENCE. BE SIR OAKHEART! BATTLE THE THING! TAKE OUT THE SEA SERPENT!

But — *seriously?* The crest over the drawbridge features two ravens. Everyone knows that Castle Crepacuore was guarded by the Ravens Three for centuries. Who designed this thing?

"It's like a walk-through attraction!" Dad's voice is filled with amazement. "Wanna do it? We still have time before your session."

I clamp my lips together hard, because even though they got the ravens wrong, so much of it is *right.* My heart wants to cross that drawbridge *so bad*, but my brain insists that someone from school will see me in there.

"That is *amazing*!" The sharp cracking voice comes from a high school kid next to me. Next to him, a woman my mom's age dabs at the corner of her eyes.

Is she *crying*?

Geek-outs lead to freak-outs. That's another one of my rules. No geeking out over the castle.

MK Nightshade is awesome, but that world isn't real. People who think it is are so lame.

I'm not lame.

So my mouth says, "Nah. Let's get to the hall. I don't want to be late," even though my heart begs me to stay behind.

2

In Hall C we finally find the room for the panel. A guy wearing a bright-blue collared shirt with an MK Nightshade Universe logo where the pocket would go pulls us aside when he spots our orange badges.

"Paul's at the front," he says, pointing to a small stage set with four chairs, a table dotted with bottles of water, and a microphone. "You'll need to check in with him, sir."

My heart pounds heavily and my throat is as dry as the Gobi Desert as we make our way to the front of the room.

I know it's not a good idea, but I turn to the empty chairs, which seem to stretch into oblivion. How many people do they expect for this thing?

"You're not Sam Marchetto . . . are you?" Another guy in a blue shirt, this one with big round glasses and hair wrapped in a messy man bun, approaches us, a confused expression on his face.

Dad stops. "No," he says.

I frown. Does this guy think that my dad—my *dad*, who

doesn't know Sir Oakheart from Rochlan the Brave — entered the kids MK Nightshade Fantastic Fan contest? He's about twenty years too old *and* he's wearing a Boba Fett T-shirt, for Yoda's sake!!

I force my dry mouth to make speech. "I'm Sam," I say.

"What?" Mr. Man Bun looks from the tablet he's just grabbed back to me.

Dad puts his hand on my shoulder. "I'm Steve," he says, slowly and carefully. "Not Sam. Sam is — "

"Sarah Anne Marchetto," I say, grabbing Man Bun's hand and giving it a firm up-down pump, like my grandfather taught me. My dry throat is gone. I'm annoyed. "It's me. I'm Sam. I'm the winner." I let go of his hand, which is damp. Ew.

It's a good thing Mr. Man Bun is wearing those glasses, because his eyes seem like they're about to pop out of his head.

"Oh. Oh. Of course. It just . . . it doesn't say — "

"Where do you need her to go?" Dad cuts him off. A deep crease appears in his forehead, like the one that he gets when he's lecturing me about the importance of finishing my homework "to the best of my ability."

Mr. Man Bun points to the table. "There," he says. "Sam is . . . uh . . . seated at the far right, closest to the moderator."

Dad gives my arm another squeeze. "I'm going to sit right here," he says, pointing at a seat in the front row. "Just talk to me if you get nervous."

Annoyance has sent my nerves on vacation. "I'm good. Thanks."

Two guys, both older than me — high school age, maybe — hover off to the side, eyeing me and Dad. One wears a BLOOD, GUTS, AND

GLORY shirt from the *Mausoleum of Monsters* movie, and the other has a Castle Crepacuore hoodie and a patchy beard-and-mustache combo that is probably supposed to make him look older but just looks scraggly. Orange badges dangle from MK Nightshade lanyards around their necks.

"Are you lost?" one says as I pass. "The Perfect Princess panel is in Hall D."

I bite the inside of my cheek and force myself not to look in his direction as I step up and take my seat in the spot labeled WINNER.

Hoodie and Guts take their seats next to me. My stomach threatens to get wiggly-nervous again, but I push it down. Man Bun puts folded cards in front of the guys. Hoodie's real name is Chris, and he took second place, and Guts — Ethan — is third. Man Bun adjusts my WINNER card, and I can't help it — I smile.

Dad's in the front row, and the guy who met us at the door holds it open as more people file in. The room is a big beige rectangle, with us at the front. Seats fill fast. There are lots of high school–aged guys. Like, *a lot a lot*. I spot a few girls, and some women who are probably around college age? Hard to tell. Everyone wears some sort of Nightshade gear: T-shirts, hats, even full costumes. Door Guy takes fake weapons and puts them aside.

Chris and Ethan talk to each other, and I squirm in my seat, tucking and untucking my tunic from under my butt, half wishing to get this panel over with and half enjoying it. I mean, I won the MK Nightshade Fantastic Fan contest! There were over 150 questions about the books, plus another fifty "identify the scene" GIF challenges for the movies. And I killed it.

But right after that thought comes another one: *You killed it—in the Super Bowl for Dorks. Good for you.* My brain seesaws between shame and pride.

Man Bun pops onto our little stage and stands in front of us, facing our table. He clears his throat.

"Guys"—he glances at me—"welcome. I'm Paul, and I'm the mod today. Congratulations on being our Boston Regional Teen Fantastic Fans. Here's what we're going to do. I'll talk first, then you'll introduce yourselves. We'll talk a little about why you like MK Nightshade, answer some audience questions, and then I have another announcement." His eyes keep sliding over to me like he's expecting me to combust or something. "Can you handle that?"

He's directing this question at me.

"Yeah," I say. Sounds easy enough. But he doesn't ask Chris or Ethan if *they* can handle it. I lean my head around Man-Bun Paul and catch Dad's eye. He gives me a big grin and a thumbs-up.

Paul moves to his seat, next to me. A few more people trickle in. I stay still, watching the audience, hoping no one from school comes in and sees me up here, but also totally aware that Chris and Ethan are whispering to each other.

Finally, when it looks like the crowd is as big as it's going to get—which is pretty darn big, actually—Paul stands and taps his mic.

"Looks like it's time to get started. Okay, everyone. Welcome to the MK Nightshade Fantastic Fan panel discussion! The three

knights . . . er, two knights and a lady . . . you see up here are winners of our online trivia challenge. I work for Nightshade, Ink, and
we're psyched to have you all here."

He goes on about the release date for the *Glut of Ghosts* movie
and a raffle and giveaway that they're doing at the big castle thing.
Then he turns to us.

"Time to meet our Fantastic Fans. Okay, guys, please introduce
yourselves." Paul turns to me.

And so does everyone else.

3

My heart feels like someone has dunked it in ice water, and the spit in my mouth is gone. I'm not sure I can talk. I open my mouth, and a weak *eegggggghhhh* sound comes across the speakers. Next to me, Chris snickers. So do some people in the crowd.

I breathe like Coach Vaughn told us to, and try again.

"I'm Sarah Anne, but online I go by S-A-M, my initials. I, uh, have been into MK Nightshade since I was a kid." A wave of chuckling goes through the audience, but now that I've started speaking it's getting easier. And I know this stuff. "Lady Althena is my favorite character from the Upper Realm, and I believe that Rochlan is really Lord Hulan, and I can prove it." I pass the mic to Chris as another murmur goes through the crowd.

It's not a popular theory, but I'd stake my winner title on it.

"Thanks, Sammy. So, I'm Chris, and I don't know who did the contest for you, because you totally don't know your stuff if you think Rochlan is the Lost Lord." I bite the inside of my cheek. Such a jerk.

When Ethan gets the mic he says that Thing is his favorite character and that he rereads the scene in the Village of Ir every night before bed. (Am I the only one who thinks a slaughter is weird bedtime reading?) He ends with the Oakheart Oath: "For fealty and light and swords that smite!" And he and Chris high-five each other. Gross. The crowd loves it, though.

"Okay, everyone, settle down." Paul takes the mic. "Now we're going to get into some questions from the audience." Immediately, people raise their hands. Door Guy passes a mic to a guy in a Lord Rochlan shirt.

"This question is for the girl in pink. You mentioned the Lost Lord already. Do you know where his character originated?"

Girl in pink?! Ugh.

Paul hands me the mic, but before I can even open my mouth, Chris chimes in — with no mic.

"Everyone knows that. Dude is Celtic, based on Irish folklore." He leans back in his chair, hands folded behind his head.

"It's *kel*-tic," I say into the mic, "not *sel*-tic, and he's based on Cuchulain, an Irish hero."

"That's what I said," Chris says. It's really not.

Ethan waves for the mic, and Paul takes it out of my hand and passes it to him. "Everyone knows Nightshade borrows from other mythology and folklore, that's how he built his world."

Another audience member: "Who would you say is the most significant character in the Upper Realm?"

Chris takes the mic. "Sammy already answered that from *her* point of view, so why don't Ethan and I take that question?"

He starts talking about the Lesser Lord, and I can't really believe what I'm hearing—the Lesser Lord is a bigger deal in the movies than in the books. Does he know *anything* about the books? Annoyance fills me.

The next question comes from a woman dressed as Lady Althena. "What do you guys think about the fan theory that all this ends with Sir Oakheart dreaming this from a cell in the castle dungeon?"

I've thought about this a lot, and I wave to Paul for the mic, but Ethan gets it first. "Can I have it?" I ask Paul. He glances at his watch.

"Sorry. We have to move on."

Now I'm so angry, I can barely see straight. I'm not getting the mic, and half the stuff these guys are talking about is *wrong*. It's like Chris watched the movies a zillion times and hasn't read any of the books or Nightshade's *Manual of Lore*. Ethan has definitely read some of the books, but mostly just certain parts over and over.

I wave at Chris for the mic, but he passes it to Ethan without even looking at me.

I don't know what to do. They're making me look like an idiot and I can't even get the mic to defend myself. To make matters worse, according to the faces of the people in the audience, they think I don't know anything about the lore either.

I resort to whispering to Paul for help.

"Paul, I need the mic."

"Next time it's your turn," he says, like I'm a preschooler waiting in line for the water fountain. Are you kidding me??

What do I do now? In the audience, Dad looks as frustrated as I feel. But as much as I want to stomp off the stage or yell or throw a fit, I am in front of a whole bunch of people that I don't know. Freaking out is not going to do anything.

Next to me, Chris has finally stopped talking. He leans back again, smugly. Ethan has the mic, and he passes it to Paul. They completely skip me.

"I'd like us to move on and do a speed-round challenge," Paul says, "so these guys — er, people of the Realm — can show us their stuff." He stands and crosses the stage to a flip chart on an easel. "I'll read the question, and you hit the table if you know the answer. We purposely made them really hard."

Annoyed and angry, I lean forward in my chair, just like Chris and Ethan. Here's where I can beat them, I know it.

"First question," Paul says. Then he peers at the audience. "No helping, you guys."

He flips the paper to the next page.

WHO FORGED THE HANDLE OF SIR OAKHEART'S SWORD? is printed there in big block letters. The audience sighs. It's ridiculously easy.

All of us whack the table at the same time.

Paul calls on Chris, who of course knows that it's the dwarf Eldwin the Younger. Chris and Ethan high-five. The audience claps. *For that?*

Next question: NAME THE FATES OF PHYRIGIA. Ethan and I hit the table together this time. Paul lets Ethan answer it.

He only gets two out of three. Finally, Paul turns to me. I fill in the third. Chris gives me a big fake smile and a "good job!" that sounds like that's not what he means at all.

It keeps going like this. Finally, after three more questions, Paul flips the chart one last time. I'm barely paying attention. The question reads, WHAT DRAGON DID ROCHLAN THE BRAVE TRAIN TO FIND GOLD?

I'm shocked that I'm the only one who hits the table.

"Sammy?" Paul looks as surprised as I feel.

I hate being called Sammy. Which I did not realize until right now.

"He trained an ice dragon that was found in the caves of Benrir," I say.

"Who even knows that, anyway?" Chris mutters under his breath. I turn to him.

"Anyone who's read the *Manual of Lore*," I snap.

Chris rolls his eyes.

"Look," he says, "the *Manual* is only backstories about minor characters and the Realm. It doesn't have anything to do with the Upper or Lower Realm time lines as we know them."

"Actually," I begin, angry, "it has a *lot* to do with them. It sets the stage for why Sir Oakheart was exiled from the Lower Realm and explains his mother's glass heart."

"Yes, but it doesn't figure into the main time line. She's not a character, so it doesn't matter."

"She's not a character in the *movies*, but she is in the books. Have you read those? 'Cause that's what's canon." My sarcasm oozes like slime.

Neither of us has the mic, and the room is deadly, awkwardly quiet. Paul slowly steps forward, arms outstretched.

"Easy there, Sammy," he says, using a voice like I'm a rabid woodland creature about to chew his face off. "You got the question right, so let's keep going. We all know the value of the *Manual*."

"Don't talk down to her!" someone yells from the audience. I am so grateful to that person.

"Even if she is wearing pink!" someone else yells.

OMG I hate everyone.

"Easy, easy," Paul says. "Let's all be respectful now."

"Yeah, chill out, Princess," Chris says softly, voice dripping with sarcasm.

Princess?! Like *I'm* diva-ing out? I throw some fierce side-eye, but I don't say anything, because what can I possibly say?

This is why I have rule number five: Don't talk Geek for long.

"Okay, that ends our speed round. Good job, team," Paul says. He blots his damp forehead. "Now, before we let you go, I have some exciting news for the three of you. Something really big. You ready?"

4

I just want this to be over with, so I can go home to my normal life of playing lacrosse, hanging out with my friends, and reading and rereading MK Nightshade books when I'm done with my homework. I do not care what Paul is going to say next.

"We are running another contest," he says. The audience cheers, but there is no way that I'm entering another contest. "Sorry, sorry," he says to the audience, "but this isn't for you. It's for these three only." He points to us.

Oh no.

"To see which of you is *truly* the biggest MK Nightshade Fantastic Fan in this area, we have created a special series of challenges and puzzles for you to complete. Should you choose to participate, you will earn points for successfully finishing challenges. The person who accumulates the most points from the contest wins a trip to WorldCon in San Diego and gets to attend a special screening of the *Glut of Ghosts* movie and cast interview, with winners from all over the US."

The movie *and* the cast interview? This might actually change everything. It would be worth dealing with whatever these jerks hand out for a little while longer.

Chris and Ethan cheer and high-five again. *Seriously?*

"There's an age restriction, right?" Ethan asks.

Is he trying to get me *disqualified*?

"Parental permission is needed since you're *all* under eighteen," Paul says to Ethan. Then, to the audience: "Another thing: There's an opportunity for interested parties to follow along with our online leaderboard. That means you can root for your favorite fan, offer suggestions on the message boards, and follow along with his—or *her*"—he gives me a sickly-sweet smile, like he's proud that he got it right this time—"progress." Everyone applauds.

And while the audience rumbles and Paul shows a slide that's a shot from a web page with our handles and boxes for challenges, Chris leans over to me.

"You think you're going to try this, Sammy?"

I shrug, not wanting to give him the satisfaction of answering.

"Your daddy won't be able to help you," he says.

"My dad didn't help!" I respond, a little too loudly. And just at that moment, the crowd settles. The mic picks up the whole thing and my words echo throughout the room. Immediately my face gets hot and I want to melt into the floor and disappear like the Lost Lord.

"All righty then," Paul goes on. "So who's excited for this group to show us their stuff?"

The audience cheers again.

"And don't worry," Paul continues speaking to the audience, "we have something for all of you too. A separate contest . . ." He explains, but I don't listen. My head throbs and blood seethes. I've been made a fool of, and I don't quite understand why.

Finally it's over. Paul thanks the crowd for coming, and we're done. It's like I've been running laps for an entire lacrosse practice, or staying up all night at a sleepover: foggy, achy, and so, so tired. I'm ready to collapse.

I didn't expect people to push to the front before we could squeeze out from behind the table. But all of a sudden, there are about twenty people — some adults, lots of high school kids — waiting to talk to us. What?

"Sam! Sammy!" A girl around my age, wearing adorable purple-framed glasses and a Lady Althena costume, waves. I beckon her to come closer.

"Hi," I say. "I hate *Sammy*, by the way."

"Oh no! I'm so sorry! Sam, then. Do you really think Rochlan the Brave is the Lost Lord?" she asks, eyes round behind her glasses.

"I do," I say, nodding, and explain how the Fierce Frost and the Darktides from *A Sea of Serpents* gave me a clue. A few other people gather around, nodding and listening.

"Totally not possible," Ethan interrupts me. He says some stuff about the ice dragons that doesn't make sense if you know the story of the Winter Wizard, which one guy tries to point out.

Some people trickle away. Purple Glasses Girl and I look at each other as he goes on and on, and I shrug.

"It's what I think."

"Well, it's wrong," Ethan says. A smug smile crosses his face. "So, you gonna do the other contest?"

My plan is to go home first and talk about it with my parents, but there's no way I am going to tell him that.

I shrug. "Maybe. You?" Dad appears at the corner of my eye. I want to get out of here.

"Of course," he says, standing up from the table. "I'll smoke you and Chris both. The tickets to that movie already have my name on them."

"Really. That's why you took third this time? 'Cause you're so good?"

Ethan scowls, then stomps away. The girl with the purple glasses stands with some friends, and she gives a quick smile as she takes off.

Chris and his scraggly beard have disappeared. Good. Another wave of exhaustion hits me and I sag into my chair.

Dad's warm hand is on my shoulder. "Good job, honey."

I tilt my head up. From this angle, he's all Boba Fett and pointy nose.

"It was awful," I say, the anger coming back. "They barely let me talk."

He crouches next to me, eyes sad. "I know."

"Why?"

23

His mouth turns down at the corners and he sighs. "Maybe because you were younger than them. Or . . ." he trails off.

"'Cause I'm a girl?"

"Maybe," he says. And from the way he says it, I know that's the reason.

I stand, ready to leave.

Paul stops us at the door. "Good job, Sammy. That was a tough crowd. Are you interested in continuing the challenge?"

I look at Dad. He looks at me and his shoulders shrug a little in an "it's up to you" kind of way.

"I don't know," I answer honestly.

"Well," he says, "you have to let me know by the end of the week, okay?" He hands my dad a card. "And, Sammy, if you do enter the challenge, no one can help you, okay? No parental involvement," he says, eyes on my dad.

"Yeah," I say, and we leave the room. Once we're in the hall, I stop and suddenly realize: *He thought my dad helped me out. He thinks I cheated!*

5

We don't say much on the ride home, and Mom and my little brother, Wyatt, are filled with questions when we get there.

"Did you win something? What'd you see? Was Chewbacca there?" Wyatt doesn't take a breath, let alone wait for my answer.

"How was it?" Mom asks.

"I don't want to talk about it," I say, grabbing an apple from the bowl on the table and heading upstairs.

"What *happened*?" Mom's voice reaches me at the top of the stairs. I go straight to my bedroom and close the door.

Flopping on my bed, I automatically reach for my copy of *A Mausoleum of Monsters*, which is on the top spot on the table next to my bed. Whenever I'm upset or stressed out, MK Nightshade is my go-to.

The words blur together and I can't focus. Right now I'm upset and stressed out *because* of MK Nightshade stuff. So should I still be reading it? I don't know. I lie there, frustrated, thinking about the awful feeling of sitting at that panel, with the boys passing the mic back and forth while I just looked like a loser.

I grab my lacrosse stick and ball, stand in the middle of the room, and toss and catch the ball while I think.

Do I take part in the next contest? Paul said there'd be "challenges" and "puzzles" to solve. Up . . . *thunk* into the pocket. What types of things would we have to do? Would the movie be worth it, to deal with those two guys again? Up . . . *thunk*. And what if I had to break one of my rules in order to do the challenges?

The thought makes my fingers tingle, and the ball clunks to the floor. I scoop it up. The rules keep my life in order—my geekdom stays hidden, separate from my school life.

I mean, unless you look really, really carefully around my room, you would never, ever know that I was even into MK Nightshade stuff: no posters, no merch. Up . . . *thunk*. On my walls are black-and-white photos of beaches that Roxy and I found at a home accessories store. (And a big poster of a rainbow over my favorite beach on Cape Cod, even though Roxy says rainbows are not sophisticated.) My bed has two well-loved stuffed animals on it: my Snoopy and Berry, a big blue bear that Penny gave me when I turned eight. Up . . . *thunk*. I have all the MK Nightshade books on my bookshelf, but so does nearly every house in the United States—in the world, probably—and the *Sea of Serpents* movie poster is my wallpaper on my computer. That's it. I like things separate, orderly. Up . . . *thunk*.

I like it so much I even have a rule for it: rule seven. Geek posters are not decor. Keep them off your walls.

Anyway, what do I care if Chris or Ethan gets to get on a plane, travel to California, and see the new movie? Or meet the cast?

Up. *Thwack* against the ceiling. *Clunk* onto the toe of my shoe. The ball shoots off under my bed, and there's a gray smudge on the ceiling where the ball marked the paint.

But they didn't win. They don't know as much as you. They don't deserve it, a little voice in my head, which sounds suspiciously like Lady Althena, nags at me as I drop to the floor and reach past the dust bunnies for the white ball.

I could be the one getting on a plane and seeing *A Glut of Ghosts* early. Maybe Mom and Dad would even let Penny take me — she's nineteen, practically a grown-up. Maybe MK Nightshade would be there, and we could talk about my Lost Lord theory. It should be me. My fingers brush the ball and I grab it, and slide out from under the bed.

"I don't think this is a good idea," Mom says after dinner. We're sitting at the table around an empty pizza box. Some soggy lettuce and croutons that escaped Wyatt's fork linger in the bottom of the salad bowl in front of us. Wyatt skipped out a few minutes ago and has set up an elaborate car race on the rug in the hall. His engine noises float into the kitchen, a mess of growls and rumbles. I should've joined him.

I drop a last bit of crust on my plate. "I don't know if it is either, but the prize is awesome."

Mom and Dad exchange glances across the table, Mom's lips pressed into a tight line.

27

"You should've seen her, Kate. She wiped the floor with these guys," Dad says. He rubs his hands together like a villain in an old TV show. "She's got the smarts."

Eye roll. What does that even mean?

"But you said they disregarded you and acted like you cheated," Mom points out. "It's only going to get worse with all the people weighing in online. I don't know that I want you exposed to trolls."

My mom knows what internet trolls are?!

Well, she kind of has a point. I didn't like what happened at the panel, and that was even *before* the audience got involved. With this next challenge, didn't Paul say that they'd be able to comment on our progress? Ew.

Dad leans forward. "This is a good learning experience, Kate. We live in a digital world, and understanding how to navigate it is important."

"This isn't the venue for learning," Mom says.

And now they're talking about me like I'm not even here. They go back and forth for a little longer, then I push my chair back from the table and stick my plate in the dishwasher.

"Where are you going?" Dad asks.

I point upstairs. "My room. I have to text Roxy about practice tomorrow."

"We are having a discussion," Mom says.

"Oh, are *we*?" I respond, extra heavy on the *we*. "I don't even know if I want to do it yet."

Mom twists her thick curls into a ponytail and fastens it with a hair tie that lives on her wrist. She clears the rest of the plates.

"You're right," she says, crossing to the sink. "Once you make up your mind, we'll have a different conversation."

That sounds great, but there's only one problem: How am I going to make up my mind? It's not like I can ask Roxy what she thinks—even my best friend doesn't know the depth of my love for MK Nightshade—and I'm sure if I asked Paul for his opinion, he'd think I should give it a try, but he'd laugh while saying it.

And I definitely know what Chris and Ethan would say: No way. Because they don't want to get beaten by a girl.

That thought brings back how they shut me down at the panel, and *that* gets me angry again.

But there is the prize: that trip to see *A Glut of Ghosts*. Meet the cast. In California.

Halfway to the stairs, I turn back and stick my head in the doorway of the kitchen.

"I'm doing it," I say, grinning. "I'm totally doing it."

I don't wait for Mom and Dad's response, just head upstairs. Grabbing my phone, I flop on the bed. There are a bunch of unread texts: about a dozen from a group text of lacrosse team members (it begins with a GIF of a baby goat; nothing important), two from Mom that she sent when I was at the Con, and eight from Roxy.

ROX: Practice at the park at 10?

And then, a little later:

ROX: Hey, where are you?

An hour after that:

ROX: You are laaaaaaame.

And then:

ROX: You there? Come on, Sarah Anne!

I scroll through the others and they are more of the same. I hadn't told her where I was going—bad idea—but I did tell her I wouldn't be around much today.

I tap the screen.

ME: Sorry. Was at a thing w my dad. Regular practice tomorrow?

Almost right after I hit SEND, the little bubbles show up. She's writing back.

Roxy and I have been friends since third grade, when we were paired as reading buddies in Miss Berry's class. Before that, all I knew about Roxy was that she was shy and the fastest runner in our grade.

She's still the fastest runner, and she's also got great fashion sense. She got me into sports—soccer, track, and my love: lacrosse—and I got her into '80s movies and MK Nightshade. For a while. We read all the books together in fourth and fifth grade, and then she switched to reading scary end-of-the-world stuff and I never left the Realm. Even though she thinks I did.

The bubbles disappear.

> **ROX:** Drills tomorrow. Bring ur mouthguard.
> **ME:** I hate the guard
> **ROX:** Better than broken teeth
> **ME:** 🎃
> **ROX:** 😐

I toss the phone onto the bed. It buzzes.

> **ROX:** So what THING were you at?

Immediately my stomach tenses. I have no plan. What do I tell her?

> **ME:** Just a thing. He asked me to come along while he did stuff.

My finger hovers over the SEND icon. I'm taking too long to respond. She can see that I've been typing! I tap it.
DELIVERED changes to READ. Nothing. No bubbles. Then . . .
Bubbles. They stop.
I take a deep breath. The message appears.

> **ROX:** 💩

What does *that* mean?

6

Mom and Dad insist that I sleep on my decision before I notify Paul, and even though I know I'm not going to change my mind, I humor them.

They also give me a list of rules:

1. ONLY GO BY SAM ONLINE/IN ANY CONTEST ACTIVITIES.
2. CHANGE MY NIGHTSHADE ACCOUNT DETAILS TO BE AS UNTRACEABLE AS POSSIBLE.
3. NOTIFY THEM IMMEDIATELY IF PEOPLE GET HOSTILE OR WEIRD.
4. THEY GET MY PASSWORDS (WHICH THEY ALREADY HAVE, BUT ANY NEW ONES).
5. DO NOT RESPOND IF PEOPLE GET HOSTILE OR WEIRD.

Dad drops me off at school and I stash my lacrosse gear in the gym locker room. Our stick bags are too big to fit anywhere else.

Coming out of the gym, I spot Tucker Hernandez and Jerry Smith. I don't want to talk to them, but before I can duck into an open classroom, I'm spotted.

"Hey, Sarah Anne," Tucker starts. He and Jerry walk on either side of me. They smell like that boy spray. My eyes water. "Where you going?"

"Homeroom, same as you," I answer. I stop myself from adding a rude "duh" at the end of the sentence, even though I totally want to. Jerry nudges me into Tucker.

"Sorry," I say, face hot.

Tucker and Jerry are the two most popular boys in our grade. Tucker knows everyone likes him, so he smiles, flutters his long, dark eyelashes, and pretty much gets whatever he wants. Practically every girl crushes on him—every girl except me. Jerry is nicer. He's almost as fast as Roxy. I can't figure out why he hangs out with Tucker.

They ask me about math homework and other stuff that they should know, and then I realize that while we've been walking, they've pushed closer and closer to me. Tucker is on my right and Jerry on my left. It's really hard to walk three across in the hall of our school with all the kids trying to get to class, but Jerry and Tucker don't budge—they just plow through the stream. I stop, and they each take two more steps forward before they've noticed I'm not with them anymore.

"What's the deal?" Tucker says.

"I gotta get a book from my locker," I say. My locker is a few halls away, and I barely use it, but they probably won't know that.

Jerry elbows Tucker, and Tucker scowls at him. "You're doing good in lacrosse right now," Tucker says. "So am I."

"Uhh . . . that's cool," I say.

"Do you know about the dance?" he says.

Uggggh. Oh no. The spring dance is in a few weeks. Is this what I think it is?

"Roxy and I haven't talked about it much," I say, which is not a lie. Thankfully, the three-minute bell rings. "Gotta go before I'm late!" I say, and jet off down the nearest corridor.

My heart pounds and my face is hot and big feeling. I don't want to go to the dance with *anyone*, let alone Tucker — and now I need to avoid him for the rest of my life. That is, if he was going to ask me. Which I hope he was not.

"Hey, girl!" Roxy comes down the hall, dressed in a blue tunic, leggings, and cute flats. Her dark hair fluffs out around a wide headband. "What'cha doing in this hall? You're gonna be late for homeroom."

"I know." In a rush, I go on. "Tucker almost just asked me to the dance, I think, and I came here to hide."

Roxy's eyes get round. "Whoa!" she says. Then she looks at her phone. "We're gonna be late. Go! I'll get you at lunch."

I go, racing through the nearly empty halls to make it to homeroom before the bell. Just as it starts to buzz, I cross into Mr. Crespo's room and am in my seat before it stops. He shakes his head, but there's a small smile on his face.

"Close one," he says.

Don't I know it.

• • •

Later, in science, I'm doodling Lady Althena's crest on one of the back pages of my notebook, then methodically coloring over it to turn it into a flower, while Mr. O'Malley goes on and on about buoyancy. Three "flowers" are done, and I draw the shield shape for crest number four. Carefully, I split it into four quadrants and begin working on the unicorn horn in the upper left section.

". . . Sarah Anne and Hugh."

I snap to attention. What? Who?

Around me, kids grab their stuff and move tables. Who is Hugh? What did I miss?

Roxy nudges me on her way to a table with Jess D., another girl from lacrosse.

"Who's my partner?"

She points. "Over there. Nerd City."

The kid has curly brown hair, wears a Kylo Ren shirt, and holds a Rochlan the Brave folder. And as I get closer . . . yes, there are ice dragons printed on his pencil. I want to burst into all kinds of questions, but I can't. He is *not* keeping his Geek on the down low, and that just breaks all kinds of my rules. I pull my gaze away from his gear.

"Hey," I say, sliding into the seat next to him.

He grunts in response, then picks at something stuck in his braces. Which are wrapped in green and blue elastics. Gag.

"Um, don't take this the wrong way," I say, trying to make the best of it, "but what are we doing? I wasn't exactly paying attention."

Hugh bobs his head, like he's half-stuck between a laugh and a sneeze. "It's for the Science Showcase," he explains. "Mr. O'Malley assigned partners this year because he said last year people didn't do enough work when they got to pick them themselves."

Oh. Science Showcase. It's one of the biggest events at the school, like a science fair, only the winners get a scholarship for a special tech camp at Chestnut College.

And it takes four weeks to do the projects.

"So, we're . . . partners?" I ask, hoping that there's been a mistake.

"We are," he says.

"Okay, everyone," Mr. O'Malley says. A glance around the room reveals that he's broken up nearly every friend group. He's even split up the White twins, who are identical, never apart, and whose sad faces are mirror images. "This is your teammate for the next four weeks. The Science Showcase is a big deal for the school and the town. You will need to come up with a project, research it, test it, and share it at our community event next month. There are specific rules. . . ."

He lists them, and I tune out.

"Is that Lady Althena's crest?" Hugh whispers.

"What? Where?" Hugh's pointing to my notebook, which I've absentmindedly opened to my doodle page. I snap it closed way more intensely than I need to.

"No. Of course not. That's so lame." My words are more intense than they need to be too.

Hugh leans back as though I've hit him. "Okay. Okay. Sorry. Just wondering." He turns away from me and faces Mr. O'Malley.

Crud. I am a jerk. I sigh, blowing a big huff of air.

Simple kindness is magic, Lady Althena says in my head.

"I'm sorry," I grumble, then face Mr. O'Malley too.

At lunch, I commiserate with Roxy and Hannah over the partner situation.

"He totally did it on purpose," Roxy says. She sprinkles shredded cheese and a guacamole/salsa mix on a mini tortilla and rolls it up, burrito style. When she bites into it, a blob of guac slides out the back and splats onto the table.

"Duh," Hannah says. "Didn't he tell your class that too?"

Hannah plays soccer and would be the typical popular girl in a TV show or movie: She's got honey-colored streaks in her hair, greenish eyes, and a big smile. She's funny too. Roxy and I have been hanging out with her a lot more this year, but I don't tell her any deep, dark secrets. Her mouth moves faster than her brain sometimes.

"At least *you* have a good partner," I point out to Roxy. I sip from my water bottle and pop a tiny tomato into my mouth.

"Truth," Roxy says. "You got stuck with the kid on the dork side. Did you see his T-shirt?" She snickers at her own joke, and although I laugh with her, my insides tighten. *I'm on the dork side too.* And I'll be queen of the dork side if I go forward with the next challenge.

It didn't used to be this way. When we were in elementary school, Roxy and I would spend hours talking about the Realm and our fan theories. But that changed the first week of junior high, when the eighth-grade girls on cross-country saw how fast Roxy could run. Those girls were popular, and jealous. But they quickly realized that making Roxy their pet project would make them look good. They added sixth-grade Roxy into their squad. And Roxy brought me along. The price of entry was giving up the Realm.

"They're not into it, Sarah Anne," Roxy told me. "And they are setting us up to lead this school. Give it up already." So I did.

Kind of.

"O'Malley paired me with a kid who smells like bologna!" Hannah complains.

"Do you even know what bologna smells like?" Roxy asks, rolling her last burrito. She doesn't let anyone get away with anything.

Roxy and Hannah bicker, and I quietly finish my tomatoes.

A lunch tray clacks down in front of the empty chair at our table. Roxy and Hannah stop, and the three of us turn.

Jess D. pulls the chair out and sits down next to me like she's been eating with us all year. I sneak a glance around: Kids at the closest tables to ours stare, waiting. Hannah and I turn to Roxy.

"I like your hair like that," Jess D. says. "You never wear it like that and you should."

I am an idiot. I hadn't said anything to Roxy about her hair, which she almost always pulls back or braids because it's so thick and kinky.

Roxy thanks her and cocks her head, considering Jess's outfit: cropped leggings and a hoodie. Roxy nods.

"Jess D. is my Science Showcase partner," she announces to me and Hannah. I want to roll my eyes at her declaration. Meanwhile, Jess D. gets comfortable and digs into her food. There's a smile threatening to break free from the corners of her mouth, like she's pleased with herself. I do not like this.

Jess D. offers Roxy mandarin oranges, Roxy's favorite, and she and Roxy chat across the table. Hannah shrugs and smirks when I catch her eye. We're on the same page, at least.

Sitting here, the contest and my chance to win seem really far away—like in another realm.

But I *do* have a chance to win.

And if I don't walk around like Hugh, wearing a Lady Althena T-shirt and carrying a million MK Nightshade school supplies, no one will even know. No one knows *now*.

"Earth to Sarah Anne! Do you read me?" Roxy knocks my foot under the table.

"Sorry."

"What happened with Tucker and Jerry this morning?"

Ugh. I'd nearly forgotten about it, and now it's going to be a thing. A *thing* in front of Jess D. I glance at her. She's all ears.

"They saw me after I dropped my stick bag off and Tucker asked me about lacrosse and if I knew about the dance." Hannah and Roxy have me repeat the whole story, exactly how it happened, at least two more times. Jess D. listens intently. Hannah peers around the caf. Tucker and Jerry are at a table in the corner with a bunch of other boys.

"What are you *doing*?" Roxy bumps her. "Don't go looking for them. Then they'll know we're talking about them." Tucker gets up from his table, and he goes over to Eloise, this sixth grader who he's been bugging for the past couple of weeks. He pulls his chair really close to her, leans over her lunch, and acts all interested in what she's eating. It makes me uncomfortable, and I turn away.

Hannah rolls her eyes at Roxy. "We *are* talking about them."

"But we don't want them to *know*," I say. "Especially because I don't want them coming over here." I don't want to go to the dance with him if he asks. Especially after that "you're doing good in lacrosse" comment. I mean, *gross*.

"I'd be soo excited if Jerry or Tucker asked me," Jess D. says, sighing. "You're lucky, Sarah Anne."

"You can have them," I say without thinking.

Roxy and Hannah freeze, staring at me. Everyone — including some of the teachers — would tell you that Tucker is the cutest boy in the seventh grade: warm brown eyes, those long lashes, brown skin, big smile. Girls swoon over him all day long.

But he's not that nice, and I don't know — he seems kind of boring to me. All he does is talk about sports. Mostly just the ones he plays. He's definitely not into a fandom — which is good, because that's not cool, but whatever. I don't know.

"You've been boy crazy since fifth grade," I say to Jess D., trying to dig my way out. "I just don't want to go to the dance with him, that's all. I thought we would go as a group."

The girls exchange glances, then turn to me.

"A group?" Roxy says slowly. "No one does 'groups' to dances anymore unless they're lame and can't find anyone to go with."

"Yeah," Jess D. echoes. "So if Tucker actually does really ask you, you'll be set. I wonder who I would go with. . . ." Her voice fades and she gets a dreamy look on her face.

Hannah frowns at me, like she's saying "Who is this girl?"

Suddenly, I wish I hadn't eaten my lunch. I hate how big of a deal this is, and now I don't want to go at all.

"Mark your calendar and get a dress," Roxy says. "You're busy on May fourth."

I want to put my head in my hands, but I can't do that.

Wait! That's the night of the *Glut of Ghosts* premiere.

And if I were watching it in California, I wouldn't have to worry about Tucker or the dance.

7

Staring at the blank message field on Penny's old laptop, I roll my head from one shoulder to the other, like I'm warming up for a game. Then I check my phone: no new texts from anyone.

Stop stalling. Lady Althena's voice cuts through my procrastination.

"Fine. *Fine*," I mutter under my breath, psyching myself up. "Let's do this."

I click on the message box and copy and paste the draft that I worked on with my parents:

To: paul@nightshadeink.com
From: sam@goomail.com

Dear Paul,
Thank you for running the panel and the contest for MK Nightshade's Fantastic Fans. I want you to know that I will be participating

in the next round of challenges, so please consider this my entry. Also note that I will be completing the challenges independently.

I am looking forward to participating in round two, and I hope I get to see *A Glut of Ghosts* in California this May.

Sincerely,

Sarah Anne Marchetto (aka SAM)

Even though the email is super repetitive, my parents wanted anyone reading it to be totally clear that I am entering the contest. I guess it makes sense, with the rude things that Ethan and Chris had said about me during the panel, but I still hated writing it that way.

I cc my parents on it, plus the Fantastic Fan email address that I received with all the info about the Con, just in case Paul or his people check that one.

I read it over a few more times, take a deep breath, and hit SEND.

Once it goes into the world, I immediately expect . . . a response. Confetti. A marching band. Something. But nothing happens. My inbox stays empty, my room is quiet. Nothing has changed.

But everything *might*.

8

I've been obsessively checking my email for days, which I never do, because other than a two-line response ("Thanks for confirming your entry, Sam! Stay tuned for next steps!"), I haven't received anything from Nightshade, Ink. Normally I wouldn't care, but I'm worried that I'll miss an important message about the next round of the contest and that the boys will get a head start. I refresh the screen again.

"Is everything okay, Sarah Anne?" Hannah asks. "Why do you have your phone?" She fiddles with her silver-and-green necklace. Silver and green are the basis of her "palette," so just about everything she wears is those colors. So Hannah.

We aren't supposed to have phones out during the school day unless there's a legit emergency at home that we need to keep tabs on while classes are in session.

To me, this is a legit emergency.

"What's up?" It's Jess D. Since she sat with us at lunch, she's been everywhere. Ugh. I'm not the only one who seems to mind, though. Hannah takes off.

I stash my phone in my locker and slam the door, spinning the dial.

"Everything's totally fine," I say, the words coming out sharp and pointy, like they want to poke Jess D. for intruding. "Just checking on something at home." I try to step away from the locker, but Jess D. blocks me. She makes her eyes big and round to seem concerned, but there's no real worry behind them.

"Oh. Really?" she says. She's trying to get something out of me.

I shoulder my way past her like I'm breaking away on the lacrosse field, only more gently. "Yeah. Heading to science!" I say over my shoulder. Before I turn completely away from her, her gaze narrows, like she knows I'm lying.

Lost in thought, I nearly crash into Hugh, who's walking with another kid that I've never noticed before.

"Sorry!" I say, doing a little dance to avoid the collision. "My bad."

"Oh, hey, Sarah Anne," Hugh says. "Do you know if it's partner day today?"

"I kind of hope not," the other kid says glumly. Hugh nods.

That further darkens my mood. I don't want to walk into Mr. O'Malley's room with these guys, but I'll look totally rude if I ditch them. So I say, "uh-huh," and keep my eyes straight ahead.

"Oh, do you know Nirmal? He just moved here last year," Hugh says.

"Hey," I say, barely giving Nirmal a smile. I don't want to start noticing him now.

"So did you hear about what happened on the *Glut of Ghosts* set last week?" Nirmal says. "The actor who is playing Rochlan the Brave fell and broke his wrist. They're thinking final production is going to be delayed. It could change the release date."

I haven't seen that at all! My heart thuds, and I bite my tongue hard to keep myself from talking. We're getting closer to Mr. O'Malley's door, and I spot Roxy out of the corner of my eye. She waves at me. Jess D. comes up to her.

I pretend not to see them so I can listen to the boys' conversation as we cross into the classroom.

"Yeah, but they're in postproduction," Hugh says. "They're just fixing a few scenes, so it shouldn't actually be that big of a deal. I think some places are reporting it to get people all hyped up. It totally worked on you!"

Whew.

They horse around, and I separate myself and head to Roxy's table. She and Jess D. are checking out bathing suits in a catalog from some mall store.

"Eavesdropping on the Geek Squad?" Roxy asks. Her eyes don't leave the pages. Jess D. grabs a yellow highlighter and circles a tie-dyed bikini.

"This would be amazing against your skin," she tells Roxy.

Roxy tilts her head. "You think so? I'll get it!"

Roxy hates bikinis. She's never worn one for as long as I've known her.

"Oh, totally," I say, agreeing too loudly. My heart thuds. "Hanging on every word."

"Huh?" Roxy finally gives me her attention, dark eyes studying me as though I'm a Science Showcase experiment. "What'd you say?"

Jess D. sighs and leans back, like I'm taking away her valuable time.

"Uh, just . . . answering your question," I stammer. *Why am I freaking out over this?*

"I don't even know what you're talking about," Jess D. says. She cocks her head and smirks at me.

"Because I wasn't talking to *you*," I say through clenched teeth. Even though I'm angry, a pinprick of fear works its way into my guts.

"I hope you weren't talking to *them* either." Roxy gives this hard chuckle after. The pinprick gets bigger, turning into a dark hole.

In fifth grade, we used to also hang out with this girl named Zoe. She moved at the beginning of last year. Zoe was deep into *Star Wars*, Harry Potter, and, of course, the Realm. But once Roxy was done with it, she thought Zoe and I should be too. And she turned on Zoe one day in the lunchroom when Zoe put her *Star Wars* lunch box on our table.

"Get that thing *away* from us. You'll make all of us look like losers," Roxy hissed.

Zoe never sat with us again, and I was too scared to say anything about it to Roxy. Or Zoe.

I guess I still am.

Roxy pulls out her homework. "We have a minute before the bell. Can you see if I did this right?"

I glance down at the paper, hoping my world stays normal. "Sure."

That afternoon at lacrosse practice, my brain won't stay focused on the day's drill. Coach Vaughn has us lined up in two rows, tossing the ball back and forth with our partners, taking giant steps back each time we successfully make a catch.

"Hey! Earth to Sarah Anne!" Roxy calls across from me. "Take another step baaaack!"

I do, and try to keep my mind on Roxy and the ball. I hated seeing her leaning over the table with Jess D., talking like I'm not in the picture.

But my head doesn't stay focused for long.

I know—just *know*—that there's a message in my inbox. I haven't checked in almost two hours. I am losing valuable time on whatever the first challenge is, I'm sure of it.

Coach stops the drill and asks us to look around. We squint at one another in the late March sunlight.

"Which pair are the farthest apart?" Her hands clasp at her waist the way they always do when she's making a point.

Jess A., who is new to the team this year, raises her hand.

"This is lacrosse, not social studies. Just say it," Coach says.

Her cheeks flame pink, but she says, "Roxy and Sarah Anne."

My cheeks should be that color. The only reason why we're doing so well today is because Roxy's been all over me.

"And why is that?" Coach says.

"Because they pay attention!" another girl pipes up. I am so not paying attention.

"Good. And . . . ?" Coach prods.

"Because they have good stick-handling skills," Raven says.

"And . . . ?"

"Teamwork!" Missy cries.

"Exactly," Coach Vaughn says. "Teamwork. That is the biggest factor here. Stick handling, paying attention . . . all that is important, but working together gets you much farther — see what I did there? — than being alone."

We nod. Coach is big on teamwork. She's always making us do drills that we can't succeed at unless we work together. And it works: We've won our division every year since I've been playing, and even before then.

"Okay, sticks on the sidelines! Let's run two fast laps to warm up!" We toss our sticks in a pile, and I tuck my elbows in and try to keep pace with Roxy, who lopes along like this is no big deal. For her, it isn't.

I hate running. It's my least favorite part of practice, but we have to do it every day. I grunt, and Roxy side-eyes me.

"You are so funny," she says. "It never gets easier?"

"Never," I pant. We come around the second turn on the field. The rest of the team trails out behind us. Jess D. is way in the back, and I'm happy about that. No one can get close to Rox when she's running. She's going slower than she normally would so I can stick with her, but my legs burn and my lungs ache. I'm at my max.

"Why doesn't it bother you during games?" She can even talk in complete sentences while she runs, which is some sort of magic. I gulp more air.

"Don't notice during games," I wheeze. In a game, I have my stick and my job: Keep someone else from scoring. There's lots of short sprints, waiting, watching, stopping. So it's little bursts of running instead of this consistent torture. My feet thud on the grass. We're halfway through our second lap. Sweat drips down my back and runs off my nose.

"You okay?" Roxy asks. I nod. We're still in front.

"Go," I say.

Without a word, she turns on the jets and pulls away from me like I'm not at a near flat-out sprint. The bright-blue bottoms of her sneakers kick up in front of me and I shake my head. She blows to the end of the run, right to where Coach Vaughn is standing, and I've still got several dozen yards to go.

Behind me, the next girl is catching up. Her breathing sounds raspy, like mine.

Inspired by Roxy's big finish, I dig down for a burst of speed. Arms churning, face tight and grimacing, I push forward as fast as I can. My lungs might explode, but I'll come in second.

Only to Roxy, though.

MOST FANTASTIC
FAN CHALLENGE
PHASE 1

9

I peek at my email the second I'm out of practice, waiting for a ride home. I was right.

Most Fantastic Fan! lights up the subject line.

I go to tap on the message. Roxy nudges me.

"Hey, 'sup?"

Reluctantly, I put the phone in my backpack.

"Just checking to see when my mom is coming," I say. We're both still in our stinky, dirty practice clothes. "All I want is a shower."

"You need one!" Roxy laughs. We lean against a brick wall at the edge of the parking lot.

Go away go away go away is the only thing running through my head. I want to open that email so badly, but there's no way I can read it with Roxy around. She'll want to know what it is, and it'll be a thing when I don't tell.

Jess D. comes over with two energy bars. She hands one to Roxy and unwraps one for herself. "Sorry," she says to me.

She's not sorry.

Roxy breaks off a piece of hers for me and we chew. When Jess D. finishes hers she says, "So, what about the dance?" She drops the wrapper on the sidewalk. So rude.

"What about it?" I kick at the piece of trash. It sticks to my shoe.

"Are you gonna go with Tucker?"

Ugh. Go away go away go away. My fingers itch. I want to check that message. I *need* to. I do *not* want to be having this conversation. Scraping my sneaker on the ground, the wrapper comes off and skitters toward Roxy.

"He hasn't actually asked me," I point out, which has the bonus of not being an answer.

"If he *does*," Jess D. says.

"He's so mean to Eloise. It makes me sad. I don't want to go with someone like that."

Roxy raises an eyebrow at me. "Who's Eloise?"

"That sixth grader that he messes with. You saw him do it today."

Roxy shakes her head. "Say yes when he asks, then I can go with Jerry."

So *that's* what this is about.

"Oooooh!" I nudge her. "You like him?"

She shrugs. "Maybe. A little."

"He's so . . ." *Boring*, I want to say. "Fast, but not as fast as you."

"It's a dance, not a race," she says. She scowls at me. "So, you gotta go with Tucker so I can go with Jerry and we'll have fun. Deal?"

I do not want to make a deal. Or a promise. I do not want to go with Tucker and I really, really hope I'm like three thousand miles away the night of the dance.

"*I'd* totally go with Tucker so you could go with Jerry," Jess D. says, all innocent but not.

Mom's car pulls into the parking lot. Relieved, I grab the handles of my stick bag.

"Later!" I say, and jog over to the car door.

"We're not done with this!" Roxy calls.

Oh yes we are.

I turn to add something, but Jess D. has stepped in between me and Roxy, blocking my view of her. Blocking other things, maybe. My heart gets heavy in my chest.

"Honey?" Mom pops the door open.

I toss my bag into the back seat, climb in, and pull out my phone.

"Hi. How was your day?" Mom says. Then more pointedly, "No phone. You just left your friends."

"It's not my friends! It's the contest. The first email came." I pop open the email app and ignore the shaking in my hands.

Hail! Adventurer SAM,

Welcome to the Ultimate Fantastic Fan Contest! There are many challenges ahead. As you complete each one, we'll calculate your total points and determine what place you're in when beginning the next challenge.

Then there's a bunch of stuff about rules that I basically skim over. I'll read more carefully tonight.

"What's it say?" Mom asks, trying to look at my phone.

"Watch the road! Nothing, yet." I keep reading.

And now, for your first challenge. This is in two parts. Click the link to go into the Forsaken Turret to complete Part I.

I click the link, but all I get is the spinning wheel of loading . . . loading. . . . There isn't enough bandwidth on the cheesy cell plan my parents bought me. *We should be almost home anyway.* And then I glance out the window. We are nowhere near home.

"Where are we going?" I screech.

"I have a couple of errands to do," Mom says. "I'm sorry, but I won't be able to feed you and your brother if we don't go to the supermarket."

OMG. I basically feel myself losing to the boys.

Mom senses my panic. "I'll drop you off at the library," she says. "They have good Wi-Fi there."

"Sure," I say sarcastically. "That and the books will distract everyone else from my sweaty self."

"Too bad," Mom says, "but at least you'll get to read your message."

I'll take being seen—and smelled—in my practice gear over losing the first challenge.

In the library, I hide in a corner study-box thing and tap on the link. There's a countdown bar while it loads, and my heart picks up speed.

And then a loud shriek comes from the phone. I nearly drop it, and every person in the back of the library turns to me, glaring, while I frantically adjust the volume.

"No cell phone use in the quiet area!" someone says.

"Sorry! It was a *mistake*," I say through clenched teeth. I finally get the noise turned down, and the other people return to their business.

An animation of the Forsaken Turret appears. It swoops into view, closer and closer on the screen, and I spot an animated Lady Althena in the window. She's doing something with her hands, her eyes on them, and it's hard to see what she's up to on the phone's tiny screen. There's a candle behind her, making the room glow. I try to do the pinch-the-screen thing to zoom in, but it doesn't work. I have to let the little movie play out, I guess.

Finally, Lady Althena finishes whatever it is she's doing. She steps to the window and tosses something out of the turret.

A bundle falls, falls, falls, out of the view of the screen and to the ground below. Then the screen changes. Animation over, a scroll appears.

Your first mission my Adventurer, is to recover Lady Althena's bundle. What is inside is for your eyes only.

Beware, however, others are coming. . . . Get to it before it is too late! (50 pts)

If you are successful, you'll commence your journey. (50 pts)

Okay . . . so finding whatever she threw out the window is going to give me fifty points, and then I do something else for fifty more. But it doesn't tell me *how* to find whatever she tossed. There's no question to answer or link to click. Instead, the scroll rolls itself up, and Lady Althena folds her arms on the windowsill and looks sadly out of her turret.

I tilt the phone. I pinch the screen.

I tap it.

Nothing.

I shake it.

"Hey, Sarah Anne!"

The voice from behind me scares me so much I gasp and let go of the phone, and it goes flying. It thunks into a bookshelf and falls to the floor. Before I can even move, Holly Yee from my math class jets over to it. Her face is crimson.

"I'm sorry! I'm so sorry!" She's saying it over and over, like she can't stop. She picks up my phone, still apologizing.

"It's fine." I sigh and take it back. Can I just do this in peace?

"Is it broken?" She's hovering.

"No, it's fine! Seriously." I glance at the screen. Same Lady Althena looking out the window.

"Oh, I'm so glad," she says, leaning over to, like, see for herself or something? I turn the screen away and catch her wrinkled nose.

I am aware of how bad I smell, thank you.

"All good," I say pointedly.

"Oh. Well, sorry. I just wanted to say hi. . . ." she trails off, like she's uncomfortable.

"Okay. See you in school." My response is flat and rude, and Holly finally leaves. Shame slides through me — I typically don't treat people like garbage (*like Jess D. and Roxy sometimes do*, a voice whispers in my head), and I hate the taste those words left in my mouth. But figuring this puzzle out quickly is really important. Anyway, she's gone.

I press my finger on different spots on the image.

Nothing.

Frustration level: sky-high.

There are about five more minutes before Mom comes back for me and I can get home and shower and get away from Holly Yee, who is probably still here.

"Do something," I hiss at the phone. Lady Althena raises her head, a puzzled expression on her face, like she heard me.

What?

"Lady Althena?" I whisper. She raises her head again. It's a speech recognition program! Now, to use the right words . . .

"*Shhh!* No cell phone use in the quiet area," a grouchy old man with a newspaper spread on the table scolds me.

"Sorry!" I whisper. This time I do head to the front of the

library, where I can talk freely. I pass Holly, who's checking out a stack of manga. I make it look like I'm video chatting with someone.

I lean in a corner between the two sets of doors leading outside, out of the way of the book-return box.

"Find it," I say.

Lady Althena still looks puzzled.

"Where is the bundle?" I ask.

She doesn't respond.

"Please show me the bundle," I beg.

This time, she gives me a smile. I'm getting closer!

"Please help me, my lady," I try.

Her smile gets wider, and the gloomy sky around the tower breaks up and turns to sun. She extends her arm to point down toward where she threw the package, and the animation perspective changes to follow her gesture.

It slides down the castle wall, past the Moat of Malice, and into a clump of tall grasses. And there's the wrapped bundle!

"Gotcha," I whisper.

10

Mom returns to the library before I've figured out how to open the package.

"Did it work?" she asks. "Were you able to solve the puzzle?"

"Hmm-mmm," I respond, not tearing my eyes from the screen. Although Lady Althena responded to speech, the bundle isn't.

I tap it.

Nothing.

I pinch it.

Nothing.

"We need to go," Mom says. "Come on."

I'm afraid my cell service will cut out on me the moment I step outside, but I have no choice but to follow her.

Mom makes me stash the phone while we walk across the parking lot — "So you don't get killed," she says — but as soon as my butt hits the car's seat, it's back in my hand.

I wake up the phone, and a faint *thump, thump, thump* sound comes from the speakers. What the . . . ?

The animation of the package in the grass is still there, but now the grass is quivering, like something—

OMG something's coming!

There must be a time limit attached to opening the package. I breathe.

Think think think, SAM. Come on! I shake the phone, hard.

The bundle lifts off the ground and splits open. Lady Althena's protective necklace, Sildir, appears. And so do a bunch of gold coins (perhaps that's where the fifty points come from), which jingle together in a satisfying way. And then there's another scroll.

I tap it.

Congratulations, Adventurer SAM! You are the first to unlock the Secrets of the Realm. Sildir is yours for protection. Keep it safe.

To continue your journey, you must solve the following riddle:

Outside a tomb, on a dark night,

One spoke with Sir Oakheart the knight.

Specify here whose words were said,

That filled the knight with such dread.

An answer box hovers below the riddle.

I read it two more times. Could it be as easy as it seems? The scene from the movie plays out in my head: Sir Oakheart meets the Raven Commander. . . .

OMG! I am an idiot. *The book is different!* There was only one obvious answer based on the *Manual* and the book version of *A Mausoleum of Monsters*.

Grinning, I shake my head. That's the trick! People are so used to the movie version, they forget that in the book Sir Oakheart never actually speaks with the Raven Commander. The Commander sent word to Sir Oakheart via messenger, but they are never together.

I tap my answer on the tiny phone keyboard and wait for the spinning wheel to tell me I'm right, so I can collect the next fifty points.

While it spins, I turn to ask Mom what we're having for dinner. But Mom is gone, and the car is parked in our driveway.

Oops.

11

"Are you hooked into the online leaderboard for the Fantastic Fan contest?" Hugh says. I nearly spit out the water I've just swigged. "You okay, Sarah Anne?"

Hugh turns back to Nirmal, who is at the table behind us.

"Yeah," he says with a shrug, "but not much is happening."

My hands shake and I drop the lid to my water bottle. It clatters to the floor.

"Sheesh, you sure you're okay?" Hugh asks. He pushes his glasses up on his nose and wrinkles his forehead.

"Yeah." I duck and grab the lid. We're supposed to be brainstorming ideas for our Showcase project, but everyone's basically been fooling around. I've been sitting with my notebook open in my lap, not doing anything except thinking about the next challenge.

Since submitting my answer to the puzzle, there's been nothing. Silence. Not an email, not a raven, not a text message. I'm beginning to wonder if the challenge was fake.

I haven't checked the leaderboard, though. I wish I had my phone with me, so I could sneak a peek.

"Has OakheartsBlade gotten it yet?" Nirmal asks.

"Not as of this morning," Hugh says. "My brother says that guy must be really dumb if he hasn't figured it out by now."

I agree. But which one are they talking about? I didn't pay attention to the guys' handles at the Con—I was too busy being humiliated.

"Turn in your list of ideas in five minutes!" Mr. O'Malley bellows from the front of the room.

Hugh swivels around on his lab stool and peers at the very white, very blank sheet of notebook paper on the table.

"Any ideas?" he asks.

"Um." I've been so focused on the contest, I haven't given this much thought. Not that I can tell Hugh that.

Hugh sighs and mutters something under his breath.

"What was that?"

"Figures," he says, and gives me a kind of glaring look.

"What's that about?" I say, heated. "You were busy talking with Nirmal. *I've* been sitting here, waiting."

"Girls aren't into science," he says. "So it figures that you'd wait for me to help you."

It takes a second for that to sink in, but when it does . . .

"Are you *kidding* me?" I say. Okay, my voice is more like a screech. "Not into science?! What kind of bull-*loney* is that? I have an A in this class. It's my best subject. I can come up with *all kinds* of ideas for this project!" I'm out of my seat, standing against the lab counter next to our table. Arms crossed. Other kids watch us. I don't care.

"Sorry! Sorry!" Hugh's face is red and his eyes dart from side to side. Terrified. *Good.*

"*Why* would you even *say* that?"

"It's just . . . I don't know. I told my brother I was paired up with a girl on this project and he . . . uhhh . . ." His voice trails off.

"Is a jerk?" I helpfully finish for him. "Jeez, Hugh."

"He kind of is," Hugh admits. "I'm sorry, Sarah Anne. I just assumed. . . ." He gives a little shrug.

"Assumed what? That I don't like science or that I'm not good at it because I play sports?"

"Um," says Hugh.

"That I can't think about problems because I straighten my hair?"

"Uh," says Hugh.

"That I'm dumb?"

Hugh stares at the floor.

I uncross my arms and put my hands on my hips.

"So now that that's out of the way, what are we going to do for our project?"

Mr. O'Malley, amused by my display in class, gives us a few extra minutes to come up with our list. Hugh and I have seven ideas, and all of them are pretty cool.

But more than the Showcase, I'm interested that one of the guys hasn't figured out the challenge yet. Everyone is in school now, so he wouldn't have a chance to work on it yet. I wonder if he's asked a friend for help.

At lunch, Roxy wants me to tell Hannah everything that happened in class. I do, making fun of Hugh the whole time, and I feel a little bad. I mean, he was a jerk, but it sounds like he's basically repeating the stuff his brother said, not any of his own ideas. Jess D., who is apparently a permanent addition to our lunch table, seems bored by my story.

Which is also pretty jerky, when you think about it.

"Have you talked to Tucker?" Hannah asks, giving me a tiny, secretive smile.

I have pretty much been making it my job to *not* talk to Tucker, but I don't want to tell her that.

"Uh, no," I say. I direct my eyes to my sandwich, not her face, like my turkey and cheese is the most interesting thing in the universe right now.

"I heard he is definitely going to ask you," Hannah says, like it's no big deal. Like she's telling me that today is Wednesday.

"Definitely?" Jess D. snorts. "I wonder if that was before or after she was partnered with the Nerd Herd for science."

A piece of bread sticks in my throat and I choke. Roxy pounds my back. I hold up my hands like I'm surrendering to get her to stop. I am the center of attention in this part of the cafeteria, and I'm mortified.

Spitting the bread into my napkin, I gasp for air. Roxy hands me my water bottle and I take a grateful swig. Before Hannah or Jess D. can say anything else, I slide back from the table and take my wadded-up napkin with its chewed-bread surprise to the garbage can.

And run into Tucker.

"Hey, Sarah Anne," he says. His big brown eyes look concerned. "Are you okay? I saw you choking."

"Fine," I say, the word coming out as a wheeze, not like a real word at all. If I were another girl, I'd probably be impressed by his bright-white smile (he got his braces off last year) or new muscles against his red T-shirt. . . . But then I get a slight whiff of BO. I toss the napkin in the garbage and turn away.

"Hey, wait —" he says.

My heart turns into a stone, falling right through my body and thudding somewhere at my feet.

"Yeah?" I don't want to respond, but my stupid mouth works faster than my brain.

"I was wondering . . ."

My face gets hot.

". . . if you . . ."

And then the bell rings and my brain comes back to life.

"Sorry! See you later!" I say, and I scamper away to my table before he can finish. I'm proud: I dodged that as well as Lady Althena dodged evil Prince Obsidian's offer of marriage.

Only I didn't resort to tossing Tucker into a volcano.

12

It takes OakheartsBlade four days to complete the challenge. Four *days*. He barely has any points, and the fans in the message boards are posting all kinds of stuff about how lame he is. Evidently, once all three of us complete a puzzle, Nightshade, Ink, posts the challenges on the site. Then everyone else gets to try solving it. And loads of them got it much faster than OakheartsBlade.

> **MNSTR356:** How lame do you have to be for it to take 4 days to solve this?
>
> **ALTHENASCROWN:** Only SAM nailed it. Nicely done.
>
> **OAKHEART79:** Dude, did you even read the Manual?
>
> **LLAMALLOVER:** Why are you in this contest?

It gets worse from there, and I close the message boards. If

OakheartsBlade keeps this up, I wonder if they'll let him stay in the challenge. Or maybe he'll quit? I'd quit if I were that bad.

I check the site and my email one more time: no new puzzle. I wish they'd give us a schedule of when they'll be released, so we know when to expect them.

My phone dings: a text from Hannah.

> **HAN:** OMG DID YOU SEE IT?
> **ME:** ???
> **HAN:** ONLINE

Hannah always texts in all caps, like she's shouting at you and everything is super urgent. She also uses a ton of random emojis, so there are horses and stars and a cow lined up at the end of her messages.

> **ME:** Where? What??
> **HAN:** ITS ABOUT YOU. CANT BELIEVE YOU HAVENT SEEN IT YET.

The leaderboard? OMG did they figure it out? Fear ices me over.

> **ME:** Stop messing w me. What?

Then another message pops up.

ROX: Article about youuuuuu!!

With a link. I lick my lips, breathe out, and click on it. It's an article in the *Auburndale Ledger* about our lacrosse scrimmage the other day. There's a paragraph about a block that I made that says that I'm "one to watch."

Big exhale.

I send notes back to both Hannah and Roxy, thanking them for letting me know. Mom and Dad will be psyched, for sure.

HAN: WANT ME 2 SEND TO TUCKRRRR??? 🐯🌴🌈
ME: I'm good, thanks.

I want to put the eye-roll emoji at the end of it, but I don't. Hannah doesn't have much of a sense of humor about stuff like that.

Instead, I flip back to the message boards. I scan through lots more people making fun of OakheartsBlade, and then a post from someone called Slayer525 catches my attention:

SLAYER525: Dudes lay off. OakheartsBlade's grandmother died. Kid had a funeral

Then there were a bunch of posts where people said how bad they felt.

It's awful that people were making fun of him while he was at his grandmother's funeral. When my grandma died two years ago,

I was super sad and missed three or four days of school. There's still an ache around my heart when I think of her.

Mentally I apologize to OakheartsBlade for thinking he should quit, then I close it all down for the night. This fantasy-world game feels too real right now.

13

I'm on my way to science class, rubbing my eyes because they're burning with exhaustion, when Roxy crashes into me. Literally.

I stumble sideways, nearly tripping, and flail my arms to steady myself, whacking Hugh's friend Nirmal in the process.

"Sorry!" I say to him, totally embarrassed. Then, "What the heck?!" I snap at Roxy. "Are you *trying* to get me to sprain a knee or ankle?" Coach would kill me if I went down: We have a big game this weekend, and I'm playing attacker.

"Sorry! I didn't mean for you to totally lose it like that," she says, and I can tell by her expression that she means it.

But I'm grouchy and her expression doesn't help. Team Nightshade hasn't released the next challenge—at least, I don't *think* they have, because the last time I looked was before last period, and that was a whole hour ago—and I've been checking my email app every second that I can. For the past two nights I even set alarms to wake up and check. I'm a refresh machine.

And I'm wiped out.

"What's wrong?" Roxy says as we walk into class. "Are you okay?"

"Tired," I mumble. "Didn't sleep well last night." I yawn for emphasis.

"Guess not," she says. "I can see your breakfast, that yawn was so big."

I shrug.

"You look *terrible*. What are you wearing?" Jess D. is not only judging my outfit, she's sitting in my seat.

For a moment, all my soupy brain gives me is Baby Bear, from "Goldilocks and the Three Bears," who has his stuff messed with for the entire story. I'm relating so hard right now.

"Yeah, what *are* you wearing?" Roxy echoes.

"Clothes," I respond to Roxy, because it's obvious I'm wearing a hoodie and jeans and didn't take the time to make myself cute. To Jess D., "Why are you in my seat?"

Jess D. gives me big eyes. "I figured it would be easier since we're working with our partners today."

"Get with your Science Showcase partners!" Mr. O'Malley calls, almost like Jess D. planned it that way. "I'll take attendance after you start working."

Scowling, I drag myself to the table, stack my arms, and plop my forehead onto them. Hugh's stool squeaks across the floor, his notebook slaps onto the table, and then something—his pencil?—taps my head.

"Hey, you in there?"

I straighten up. "Barely. What are we supposed to be doing?"

He frowns at me. "Don't you ever pay attention?"

"Didn't we already have this argument? And didn't I already win it?" Being annoyed perks me up.

Hugh pulls our idea list from his folder. A piece of paper falls out and I scoop it up for him. It's a ticket stub from a Red Sox game. I hold it out to him.

"Truce. You went to Opening Day?"

Hugh nods and takes the ticket from me. "That's why I missed class the other day," he answers. "I go with my grandfather every year."

I hadn't noticed he was gone.

"That's cool. I've never been to Opening Day," I say, "but I go to a few games with my mom every year. We listen to almost all the home games."

"Listen?" Hugh's forehead creases.

"Yeah. We have cable and stuff, but my mom likes to listen to the games on the radio. She got me and my sister and brother into it. It's our thing." My cheeks get hot.

"That's so cool!"

"Cool better be about your project," Mr. O'Malley says as he comes past our table.

Conversation over, I grab my stuff from my backpack. Across the room, Jess D. raises her eyebrow at me. The expression on her face basically says, *oh, hey, got a thing for Geek Guy?*

I give her a dirty look back, but I'm all business now.

"We need to put together a materials list for our project," I say. The plan is to calculate the energy found in different foods by recording the amount of heat each one gives off. I like it 'cause it goes with my sports thing; Hugh likes it because we get to set stuff on fire.

"We need food, obviously," he says. I don't even bother responding. "What type of food do we want to test?"

"Junk food versus healthy stuff?" I suggest. Seems like a no-brainer.

Hugh wrinkles his nose. "That's almost too easy," he says. "Everyone would expect us to do that. Let's be different."

Now I'm nose wrinkling. "It's a science fair project, Hugh. How different can we be?"

Around us, some kids are deep in conversation with one another, and some lab partners aren't doing anything at all. Roxy and Jess D. huddle over Roxy's notebook. They're building catapults or something. I'm not supposed to know—Showcase projects are secret until everyone's initial reports are turned in—but I saw some sketches when I flipped through her notebook the other day, copying down the homework assignment.

I kind of wish we'd thought of a catapult.

"What if we burned all of one type of food, to find out which is the best?" Hugh says. "Like, different flavors of potato chips? Then we can find which potato chip has the most energy." I guess that's different enough.

"Sure."

We decide to focus on one brand, testing all their crazy flavors— including dill pickle.

Hugh scribbles away at our materials list while I work out how we'll measure the heat from the burning chips. There's no way I am going to talk to him again this period, now that I know I'm being monitored. Default: science snoozefest. I finish setting up the equations we'll need and yawn so wide my jawbones pop.

Then my phone buzzes in my pocket. I sneak a glance at the screen.

1 New Message: Nightshade, Ink

Naptime. Is. Over.
It's game time.

14

I ask for a bathroom pass and take Mr. O'Malley's life-sized plastic human femur with me to the nearest girls' room. To be on the safe side, I close myself in a stall and lock it. Why do they release these challenges during the day? All three of us are in school and they know it.

They're messing with us, and I want to win, so I fall for it. Gotta take any chance I can to get ahead of the boys.

I open the email app and there it is: "Nightshade, Ink," in the "from" field. My heart skips a beat, and my hands shake so much that it's hard for me to tap the screen in the right place.

Finally the email opens. I can tell it's graphics-heavy, though, because there are all these empty boxes on the page and the thinking wheel spins at the top of my phone screen.

I really, really hate our cell phone carrier. And these stupid brick New England school buildings. It's like they were designed for bad service.

"Come on, come on, come—" The door to the bathroom bangs open. *Did whoever it was just hear me talking out loud?*

And then the person chooses the stall next to me.

Ugh. Who *does* that? It's, like, an unwritten rule: In a bathroom with three stalls, you start by taking the one farthest away, next person takes the one at the other end, leaving the middle empty. It's common courtesy.

Most of the stupid challenge graphics won't load, and, based on the elaborate designs that *have* loaded, most of the text is actually found in the images.

The toilet next to me flushes.

I need to go back to class before Mr. O'Malley—or Hugh— sends a search party.

Loadloadloadloadloadload . . .

"Sarah Anne? Is that you? Are you okay?"

It's Hannah.

"Um, fine! I'm totally fine." I take another look at the screen— still loading—and stuff the phone into my pocket. I flush and grab the pass, then step out of the stall.

"How'd you know it was me?" I ask. Hannah's leaning over one of the sinks, reapplying lip gloss in the mirror.

"Your shoes. No one except Patty Rodriguez has a pair like that."

No one else has a pair of purple high-top Chucks? *Really?*

How long has Hannah been paying attention to my footwear? While I'm busy figuring that out, I catch my reflection in the mirror.

Not that the industrial lighting is doing me any favors, but Jess D. is right: I look awful. There are dark circles under my eyes, my skin looks gray—even my ponytail is off center. I try to straighten it, then give up and take it out, splash some water on my face, and blot with a scratchy paper towel.

"Are you okay?" Hannah asks again. She turns away from the mirror. "Want some?" She holds out the lip gloss.

"No thanks. I don't think it's going to help." I laugh a little.

Hannah frowns. "You know you can talk to me, right? If something's wrong?"

Ugh. You can't talk to anyone who says that. Not that I'd be lining up to confide in her, anyway.

"I'm fine," I say, not meeting her gaze. I crumple the paper towel and toss it into the trash can. Hannah hands me the femur. She came from Miss Vogel's class: Her pass is a fake sunflower.

Hannah's eyes narrow. She doesn't believe me; I can tell.

"Just tired," I say. My heart pounds and my hands sweat. I want to get away from here. "Gotta get back to class." I push past her and yank open the door, annoyed that she found me, annoyed that I can't check on my downloading challenge, annoyed that I'm involved in this stupid contest to begin with.

And really, really annoyed that I want to win so badly.

"Feel better!" she calls out in a singsongy voice.

"The second challenge was released!" Hugh whispers to Nirmal as I go to sit down on my stool. I'm so startled, I nearly miss the seat, and I crazy-flail to keep my balance, whacking my left hand on the science table really hard. *Really* hard. Tears fill my eyes and my fingers sting, but I don't care.

"Sarah Anne, you okay?" Behind his glasses, Hugh looks worried.

"I'm fine. Just . . . go back to what you were doing," I snap, trying to cover up my awkward spill and his annoying question.

How did he know? That's what *I* really want to know.

"You get an alert?" Nirmal asks. His Science Showcase partner is asleep, facedown, in his notebook. Not even pretending to hide.

Hugh nods. I'm trying not to look at them directly, playing it cool by flipping through my notebook and glancing up at the board, where Mr. O'Malley has written the time line for the Science Showcase projects. Carefully I copy each item.

"I signed up for text alerts," he says. "They send them when the challenges are released, when each player opens the message, and when they solve the puzzle—and then when it goes live for the rest of us. Sam already opened his."

I am not copying notes anymore.

As a matter of fact, my timeline now reads:

1. TURN IN MATERIALS LIST

2. SET UP LAB SHEETS

3. DESIGN CONTROL AND EXPERIMENT GROUPS

4. BEGIN EXPERIMENTS

5. OPEN THE MESSAGE

6. SOLVE THE PUZZLE

Hugh cracks up. He's peering over my shoulder at my notebook. I snatch it to my chest.

"Sorry!" he says. "But Sarah Anne, we weren't talking about this assignment, so don't stress about that stuff. It has to do with this contest thing that Nirmal and I are into."

"Oh yeah," I say, tossing my hair like I don't care. In the corner of my eye, Roxy is giving me a *look*. "What's the contest?"

Hugh and Nirmal glance at each other.

"I'm not going to make fun of you," I say, trying to say it in a way that means I *could*, but I won't. *Please tell me please tell me please tell me . . .*

I need to know what they know. Especially about the text thing.

Nirmal looks skeptical, but Hugh shrugs. "Fine. Have you ever heard of that book series . . . the MK Nightshade *Realm of Heroes*? They make movies out of it?"

I twirl a piece of hair around one finger, like I am not all that interested in what he's saying.

"Oh yeah. I think so."

"Well, they're having this contest to identify the best fan or whatever, and there're kids competing for a chance to win passes to the new movie premiere and a cast interview."

"Competing?" I say. Mr. O'Malley comes by and the three of us retreat to our notebook pages.

Mr. O'Malley goes to the next group of kids. Hugh gnaws on his ice dragon pencil. "Yeah. They solve puzzles and do all these challenges. Everyone thought part one was done, but they just released a bonus challenge."

"Oh," I say, still acting disinterested.

"Yeah," Hugh says. "Anyway, I'm really into it because my brother is one of the contestants."

15

For the second time today, I nearly fall off my lab stool.

"Your *brother*?!" It comes out more like an accusation than the "cool, casual" vibe that I'm going for.

"Yeah, it's pretty rad," Nirmal butts in. His lab partner has finally woken up and blinks at us. "He's in second place, behind this kid named Sam."

Who even says rad *anymore?*

The corners of my mouth threaten to break into a smile. I try really, really hard *(thinkofsadkittens thinkofsadkittens)* to hold it together, but now I have a zillion more questions, including who Hugh's brother is. Is it Ethan? Chris? How do I ask him without giving away why I'm interested?

The bell buzzes and Mr. O'Malley collects our project lists. Hugh and Nirmal leave, not adding any more to the story.

But now I've got a whole other puzzle to solve.

Besides the one in my email, which I still need to read. What if the boys are already working on it? And what if, even worse, they've already solved this one?

"Hey!" Roxy bumps into me again.

"Hey." I'm in the hall outside science class. I'd totally zoned out and have no idea how I got here.

"You took your hair down," Roxy says. She's giving me a playful grin, but I don't feel like giving one back.

"It didn't look good," I respond.

"Definitely not," says Jess D., who materializes on the other side of Roxy.

"Thanks, cheerleader." It's rude, but I don't care. Jess D. goes off in a huff.

"Cold, Sarah Anne. What's up with you?"

"I told you, I'm tired," I say rudely. I just want Roxy to go away.

"Yeah you are," she says. She stalks off, just like Jess D.

I race through the hall to my next class, language arts, and drop into my seat. Quickly I whip out the phone, hide it in a book like I'm reading, and open the email app again.

A few more of the images have loaded, but not all of them.

But the images don't make any sense. There's a piece of a hand. Then a part of a crown. Part of Sir Oakheart's blade. Then a few blank ones. Then part of a dragon.

I don't know what to make of it, not at all. The thought makes me worry. If I can't figure this out, I'm sunk.

There are no words that I can see yet.

Around me, other kids fill the chairs. The bell is going to ring in a few seconds, and if I don't put the phone away, my teacher is going to *take* it away. The wheel spins as the phone struggles to download the graphics-heavy message, but the bell buzzes before it makes much more progress. Frustrated, I stuff the phone back in my pocket and scowl.

As Miss Walker takes attendance, my brain won't leave the images alone. What are they?

I sketch out a grid of nine squares on a fresh sheet of notebook paper, then label each one with the image in the grid. It looks like one of those plastic slide-'n'-click puzzles that you sometimes get as a birthday party favor when you're a kid.

Wait—Is that what it is?? A slide-'n'-click? I wonder if I can drag and drop the tiles like one of those puzzles that makes a larger image when you're done.

"Sarah Anne! Sarah Anne!" Miss Walker's voice brings me back to earth. I have to bite my tongue so that I don't answer with an MK Nightshade quote or something.

"I'm so sorry," I respond.

Apologies are getting to be second nature.

16

I have never hated going to lacrosse practice until today.

First, Roxy said my hair is supposed to be in French braids down the side, evidently, not a side ponytail. Whatever. I'm leaving it; I don't care.

Then, Coach Vaughn had us pair up, and since Roxy is still ticked about my blow-off after science, I'm stuck with Olga, who moved here last year from Russia and doesn't really understand lacrosse, but is a fantastic blocker.

We're tossing the balls and stepping back, just like we always do, only unlike the way I always do, I'm dropping the ball everywhere. Olga scowls at me as it hits my foot and rolls halfway to the sidelines, where our gear is stashed.

"Focus, Marchetto, focus!" Coach calls.

I'm trying to, but all I can think about is that puzzle.

I toss the ball to Olga, and my throw is wild. She scowls again and goes trotting off after it.

Every other pair has moved several steps apart, and Olga and I are now the closest together. Jess D. and Roxy are as far apart as Egypt and Peru, of course. Now it's my turn to scowl.

When Olga comes back, I force myself to lock in and focus. With a few tosses, we're closing in on Roxy and Jess D. Olga's expression is still dour, however.

A few drills, then we scrimmage.

Finally. Sprinting back and forth across the field, staying with my player, forces me to pay attention to the now.

I can't think of the stupid contest when I'm getting in the way of another girl or vying for the ball and shouting to Jess A. to catch her attention for a pass. Even though there are a dozen other girls on the field, lots of times I feel like it's just me and my stick—alone.

And then we're done. My hands ache from gripping the stick and my back and legs are sore and bruised. But once my body is still and my brain stops tracking the other players, it clicks back into stress mode.

I still haven't seen all of the puzzle! What if the boys already finished it?

I change quickly and don't even wait for Roxy at our gym lockers. Instead, I race outside and telepathically beg my mom to show up soon.

I sneak a look at my phone. There are the instructions! And more of the images. Hooray for the power of ridiculously slow cell service.

I tap on the message and it pops open:

Congratulations, Adventurer! You have reached the next stage in our journey. Below, piece together the map to the location of Benrick the Elder's tiny hut, and therein you shall find great treasure.

But beware: Once the map is assembled, you will have only three hours to follow it to Benrick's hut. Fare thee well, hearty Adventurer!

So I was right — it is a slide-'n'-click — but then how am I going to follow a map to a pretend world to find treasure?

I'll have to deal with that later.

"Hello, Adventurer!" Roxy says in a deep voice.

I almost drop the phone. How long has she been looking over my shoulder?

"What?" I say. "Do you knock?"

"Uh, we're outside, genius. . . ." Roxy says. "What is that, anyway?"

Think fast . . . faster.

"It's some app that my brother downloaded on my phone," I say, sliding it into my pocket and away from her prying eyes. "I keep getting these annoying alert messages from it." I smile, hoping I don't look as panicked as I feel.

"What's the app?" she says. "It looks cool."

Roxy's really into gaming, which I always forget. She plays against all these guys online and trash-talks them and stuff. She's pretty good too.

I shrug. "Dunno. Some sword-fighting thing. Your mom picking you up today?" Hoping I can change the subject.

"Grandma," Roxy answers. "Hey, show me the email. I'll do the unsubscribe for you." She holds her hand out for my phone, which I absolutely am not going to give to her.

"Umm . . . uh . . . well, I can't. My brother, um, needs them. He likes to see them for the tips for the game and stuff." My lies come easier and easier.

"Those things are just spam and they can even slow your phone down with all the graphics. Let me show you how to switch to a plain view."

Why does Roxy have to be so interested in my tech savviness?

"It's totally okay," I say. "Forget about it." The phone is deep in my pocket and it's not coming out.

"Hey, Butterfly!" Jess D. flits over. Roxy giggles.

"Hey, Dragonfly!" she answers. They both laugh.

What the . . . ?

They must see the confusion on my face. Roxy stops giggling.

"We were messing around during drills," she says.

"They're like nicknames," Jess D. fills in helpfully. Not.

"I get what they are," I say.

"Awwww, jealous?" Jess D. coos. I would shoot daggers out of my eyeballs at her if I could.

"No way," I say to Roxy, ignoring Jess D.

There is no way Roxy believes me. I don't even believe myself.

BONUS CHALLENGE

17

I tap at the puzzle as soon as I get in the car, trying to put it in some order. The pieces don't make sense, though—there's no way they can create a full image once they're assembled.

And then, as I slide the hand near the sword, gold sparkles appear on the screen and the two images combine and animate—the hand grabbing the sword.

Ah! Got it. So the more pieces I fit together, the clearer the picture becomes. I just have to figure out the right combination of images.

Which has to wait until I get home, because of the cell service. Frustrated, I bang my head against the seat.

"Hi, honey," Dad says. I hadn't even realized he was the one who'd picked me up.

"Hey. Sorry," I say. "Why are you here?" Dad works in Boston at a company that manages a bunch of assisted-living places.

"Had a meeting out here," he answers. "Didn't have to go back to the office when it was done. But this is about you. Another puzzle?" he asks. "Or a fashion emergency?"

I roll my eyes at him. "Very funny. It's another puzzle. A literal one." I explain how it works. He nods and looks thoughtful.

"So it's all about relationships," he says.

"I guess."

"How the two items are connected. Obviously, the sword and the hand go together. What other images are there?"

I list the other images that loaded: the dragon, the crown, a castle, an eye, two birds. The others are still blank.

He listens carefully. "Think about how they're related," he says. "Even in ways that you don't expect." We pull into the driveway.

"I'm thinking about getting on the Wi-Fi," I say. I bolt out of the car.

"Hey, Adventurer!" he calls. "Don't forget your gear!"

I trudge back to the car and grab my bag. He wishes me good luck, then the phone vibrates.

ROX: WTH is up w you? You were so rude.

I'd thrown my stuff in the car so fast to get out of the conversation that I hadn't said goodbye.

ME: Sorry. Just preoccupied w stuff.
ROX: We still getting together tomorrow?

Shoot. I'd forgotten that we'd made plans. Even if the game sends me to the Loch of the Lost, I have to find a way to get back to hang out with Roxy tomorrow.

ME: TOTALLY.

While Roxy sends me details, I open my laptop and log in to my email.

The message won't open.

What?! Have I already missed the window to solve the puzzle?

A text box pops onto my screen.

IP ALERT, it reads. CHALLENGE MAY ONLY BE EXECUTED ON MOBILE DEVICE.

My phone?! I have to finish it on my phone?!

It buzzes again, with another text from Roxy.

And then Hannah sends a group text to me and Rox.

HAN: Fashion emergency! Which shoes?

Three pictures are attached.

I want to bang my head against the wall. Instead, I select one, then turn on the Do Not Disturb feature, open the email app, and go back to the puzzle.

It takes me an hour and a half of clicking, sliding, tapping, and waiting for my ancient phone to load, but when I slide the eye next to the birds, the final gold sparkles appear.

The image on my screen looks nothing like the puzzle pieces. It's a map to Benrick the Elder's tiny hut, just like it said in the instructions.

And a big green button below it that reads GO.

18

I check my battery life: 68 percent. That should be okay, I think. I hope. It needs to last for three hours at most, right?

I press the green button.

Another text box pops up: *Adventurer! You must be able to finish what you begin. Are you committed to this quest?*

YES and NOT NOW buttons appear.

I bite my lip. *How long will this take? Will I have enough battery? Am I going to have to drive somewhere? What if I can't finish? What if I lose service in the process?*

I stand outside my bedroom door, weighing all the options. But the one thing that keeps coming back to me is: *If I don't do it, I could lose.*

And after listening to Hugh and Nirmal, and knowing that Hugh's brother is one of the other contestants, there's no way I will let anyone else beat me in this game.

I tap YES.

Immediately, the map zooms in and my phone squawks "Let us begin" in Sir Oakheart's voice.

"Proceed north to Beggar's Cave," he orders.

Um . . . ? Which way is north? And there's no Beggar's Cave in my house — Beggar's Cave is on the side of the Mountain of Shame in the Lower Realm.

"Proceed north to Beggar's Cave," he says again.

I step forward, staring at the phone screen. The screen turns to a Lower Realm path. I get it — kind of. It's going to make me walk in real life, but show me the Realm on-screen. So I'll walk around the neighborhood, I guess, and the phone will take me to the cave.

Following the instructions is easy: I go down the hall, downstairs, and outside. My screen scrolls through the woodsy Lower Realm path. It's autumn there, and the leaves fall gently from the trees. Here, the chill of winter lingers in the air.

"Proceed west to the River of Tears."

Sir Oakheart, we have a problem. I'm standing in front of my neighbor's house. And although the Gerrys are nice — we have a BBQ with them every summer — I'm pretty sure they don't want me trekking through their kitchen on my quest.

"Proceed south to the River of Tears."

My options: Go through the Gerrys' house or walk around it and hope the instructions pick up behind it. I glance at my phone one last time.

"Sarah Anne! Hey!"

I whip my head around. It's Rob Hingham, our neighbor. He's a senior in high school, a friend of Penny's.

He also has the most ridiculous cleft chin and best smile ever. And he's nice, not like Tucker. My knees go weak.

"Uh, hey," I say. My mouth goes dry and I lick my lips. Stuff the phone into my pocket.

"What's up?" he asks. "How's Penny liking Emerson?"

I stammer something, and then, from my pocket I hear:

"Proceed south to the River of Tears."

"What's that?" he steps closer. He's wearing his MUSTANGS BASKETBALL T-shirt and smells like sweat. I step back.

"Nothing. Just a game," I say. "Uh, Penny's coming home to visit soon." It's hard to keep track when your heart's pounding and you can't pull your eyes away.

"Proceed south to the River of Tears."

"Um, bye!" I say, and I speed walk around the corner of the Gerrys' house, into their backyard. Only when I'm there do I pull out my phone.

On-screen there is a giant blu bear—the worst of the wild beasts in the Lower Realm. He's sleeping in a pile of leaves. Right in front of me.

My legs quiver as if the creature were right in front of me. I mean, it *is*, just not in real life.

In real life I'm next to the Gerrys' bare garden.

What now?

Turn back?

I experiment by slowly turning around. The woods disappear, and a gray void appears.

Aren't you committed to the quest? floats onto the screen. Curses.

I turn back to the bear. It's still sleeping, curled up in a ball the size of a small car. Carefully, as though I really am walking on twigs and crunchy leaves, I take a big step to the side and draw my other foot over.

The view shifts as though I've stepped to the side of the bear. I can only see the front half of its body.

It snores, and the sound makes my phone vibrate. I jump, and so does the phone.

The bear opens one eye.

In the Gerrys' backyard, I hold my breath and stare at the screen. It watches me. I don't dare move. My heart bangs in my chest like I've just run ten laps in lacrosse.

Suddenly a sparkle of gold lights up the bottom right corner. I peer at the spot. It's a berry bush.

Slowly, carefully, I crouch down, as though I actually am in the woods, going to grab the bush. I reach out my hand—wait, not that hand . . . it needs to be the one with the phone in it—and, on-screen, a gloved hand grabs the plant. Slowly I pull it out of the ground.

The blu bear's head is up. It's roughly the size of the small table next to our couch. I toss the bush to it, a low, gentle underhand, and it lands right in front of its paws. It bends its head down to sniff, then starts eating.

I know a chance when I see it. I walk, quickly, purposefully, back to where I think the path is.

Right in front of the Gerrys' kitchen window.

Some thick vines block my view, but I push through and feel a wave of very real relief when I see the path in front of me.

"Proceed south to the River of Tears," Sir Oakheart says. I resume, hoping to avoid any more surprises.

19

By the time I find Benrick the Elder's tiny hut, I'm two streets over and standing behind someone's rhododendron shrub, with 22 percent battery and cuts and scrapes from pushing through a hedge between two yards. I can't believe no one has stopped me or said anything, but maybe they're just shaking their heads at the girl staring at her phone, not paying attention to her surroundings.

Or they could all still be at work.

Anyway, here I am. I knock on the hut's door by tapping the screen. It opens, and Benrick comes out.

"Huzzah! Greetings, weary traveler, come inside," he booms.

When will this end? I have to figure out how to get home for my real dinner, not hang out with Benrick and drink mead. But I've come this far.

I enter the hut.

It's lit by flickering torches and is kind of hard to see on my phone screen. Benrick leads me to a small table and we sit.

"You are the first one here," he rumbles. "As such, I have gifts for you."

I won?! Again?

Meanwhile, Benrick has pulled out a leather satchel. He removes several items.

"Gold for your time," he says, placing a stack on the table.

"Mead to toast your cleverness," he says, adding the bottle to the tabletop.

"And bread for your belly." A loaf joins the other objects. My real-life belly grumbles.

The winner message pops up, with an added note that this concludes part one of the challenge. Relieved, I stick the phone in my pocket.

And come face-to-face with a little old man, peering at me through the leaves.

"Why are you in my rhododendron?" he asks.

Oh man . . .

20

Roxy fusses with the pillows on her bed. She's got about a dozen of those small throw pillows, all in various shades of purple, and she's putting the round ones in front and the square ones in back.

"You're just going to take them all off tonight," I point out. "Just leave it and let's go before it rains." We're going to the park near her house to play lacrosse catch and then grabbing lunch.

"I like how it looks. And oh, ya know, since it's going to rain, I figured we could just skip the park. Jess wants to meet up at the mall." She doesn't look at me while she's talking. She knows.

I don't say anything. I've been tricked. It's . . . what do you call it—when you think one thing is going to happen but you get something else instead? A bait and switch.

"I thought it was just us," I finally say quietly.

"It'll be fun." Roxy finishes her artful pillow positioning. Angry, I picture myself launching my body headfirst into the pile, purple stuffed fabric flying into Roxy's color-coordinated, organized bedroom.

I text Hannah.

ME: Can one of your moms drop you off at the mall? Shopping w Rox + Jess D.

HAN: Think so. Need rescuing? 😶 ☠️ 🥊 💥

ME: Something like that. 😒

At the mall, Jess D. decides that we need to pick out headbands. "Matching is just *lame*," she points out. "But *coordinating* is totally different." Hannah's is green and silver, of course. Roxy's is orange.

I like a blue-and-purple one, so I'm in the club.

We're sitting on a bench outside the pretzel shop, sharing a cup of warm pretzel nuggets because Jess D. says there are too many carbs in a container for one person. I don't care about carbs.

When did Jess D. become the one to decide everything?

"Check that out," Roxy says, her voice loaded with sarcasm. "Nerd Herd, coming through."

She's pointing at a big group of kids standing outside FanWear, this new store that has merch from all kinds of comics, TV shows, movies, etc. There's a banner hanging above the door with *Wear your Realm* printed on it.

New merch??

Normally they email the fans to say they're releasing new stuff, and I browse online. I guess I missed the message. Since I'm here, though, I kind of want to see what's up. How can I check out what's going on without taking Roxy, Jess D., and Hannah with me?

Hannah shakes the paper cup at me.

"This one's yours, Sarah Anne," she says. She checks her phone. "My mom's here. I gotta go." She grabs her stuff.

"Which mom?" Jess D. asks, like she's curious. But the expression on her face is not innocent. It's sly.

"Does it *matter*?" Hannah snaps. She looks at me. "Have fun this afternoon."

I want to say something to Hannah and tell Jess D. to knock it off, but inside I'm a mix of I-don't-know-whats and I'm-scared-tos. Hannah's moms are super nice and I like going over there, and as I get up the nerve to say that, she's gone. Roxy looks the same way I feel. Then she turns to Jess D.

"Hannah's moms are awesome. Don't be a jerk."

Jess D. ignores Roxy and lazily looks in the pretzel bite cup. "Oh, there's one left. We can split it three ways so it's fair."

Roxy cocks her head. "Jess, that's ridiculous. The thing is too small to split. Someone should just eat it."

"But then it won't be *equal*," Jess wails. Only she would get dramatic about pretzel bites.

While she and Roxy argue, I push away the sick feeling I have about the Hannah thing, grab the last two bites, pop them into my mouth, and pluck the cup from Jess D.'s hand — enjoying her shocked expression the whole time.

"Gotta throw this out!" I say cheerfully. There's a garbage can on the far side of the bench, close to where Roxy is sitting, but there's another one across the mall boulevard from us — right in front of FanWear.

This is my chance.

Without looking back, I cross the space and head for the garbage can, not paying attention to anything else. It's like I don't even see the mob of geeky kids or the big poster.

I toss the cup in the trash, and then, as I'm about to scope out what I can on the down low, I hear: "Sarah Anne!"

It's Hugh. And Nirmal.

They're in the mob, waving and gesturing for me to come over to them.

I know—I *know*—I shouldn't go over there. Jess D. and Rox are watching my every move. But I can't help it. These guys will know what's going on with the store.

I cross my arms, trying to look disinterested and cool.

"What's up?" I say. "What's all this?"

"New Nightshade merch," Hugh says. He's so excited he's practically shaking. "They haven't released anything official since last April."

Actually, it was May, but whatevs.

"So, you're in line for T-shirts?"

Nirmal frowns. "That's not what this is about," he says. "It's really cool. . . ."

"Yeah," Hugh jumps in. "Since Sam won the first two challenges of the Fantastic Fan contest, they're releasing stuff early *and* a limited-edition Lady Althena hoodie!"

What the . . . ?

"Really?" I say. I'm trying to keep cool, keep calm, hold it

together, but this is *so* amazing. I made something happen in the Nightshade realm!

"Sarah Anne!" Jess D.'s shrill voice cuts through the crowd. She and Roxy are standing several feet away from me, as though they'll catch something if they come any closer to the group of kids.

"Gotta go," I say. "Good luck getting the merch."

When I get back over to the girls, Jess D. glares at me. And then stalks away so that Roxy and I have to follow her. She stops once we're around the corner from the crowd, out of eyesight.

"What was *that*?" she snaps.

"What are you *talking* about?" I mimic her tone. *What is her deal?!*

"You're kidding me." She puts a hand on her hip like she's in a TV show and gestures to Rox. Rox just shakes her head.

"Give me a break," I say. "He's my Science Showcase partner."

"He's a total dork," Jess D. says, like it's the most obvious thing in the world. "And Tucker will never ask *you* to the dance if you hang around with him. But *I'll* be ready."

Good.

21

"Delivewy! Delivewy!" Wyatt yells. He loves when mail comes to the house. "There's a delivewy!"

I leave my spot on the couch to help him open the front door, otherwise he'll just keep shouting. There's a brown package on the porch, one of those packing-envelope things, and I flip it over to see who it's addressed to.

Me.

And the return address is Nightshade, Ink.

Whoa.

"Is it for me?" Wyatt says. He's hanging on my arm and I shake him off.

"No," I say. My voice reminds me of Jess D.'s from the mall. His face falls. He can be annoying, but overall he's a good brother and I feel kind of bad.

"But you can help open it," I offer instead. His big brown eyes shine with his smile and he happily leads me to the kitchen counter and the scissors.

What is this? Does it have to do with the next task?

We cut the envelope open. There's a piece of parchment-like paper right at the top. It's printed in swoopy, swirly Nightshade font.

Congratulations, Adventurer! Similar to Benrick the Elder, we want to share some gifts with you to celebrate your achievement. Please accept these tokens of our appreciation and admiration.

But remember: Some gifts come with great responsibility.

Inside is a soft object wrapped in plastic. I pull it out.

It's a rich midnight-blue hoodie with Lady Althena's crest on the back—it must be the one Hugh was talking about at the mall. The fabric is soft and thick, perfect for early spring weather, and I love it.

Too bad I'll never wear it out of the house.

"What else is in there?" Wyatt asks. He's unimpressed by clothing.

"That's it," I say, and turn the envelope upside down. "See?"

Another piece of paper floats to the floor.

It's a coupon, redeemable for a smoothie and a sandwich at a nearby lunch place. *Benrick the Elder* is scribbled on the *from* line. I get it—the "mead" and the "bread." And the hoodie must be in place of the gold.

This is also disappointing to Wyatt.

"I'll take you with me," I tell him. "We can have smoothies together."

That he likes. He goes off to play with his cars, evidently satisfied.

Alone in the kitchen, I thread my arms through the sleeves and slip the hoodie on. It's cozier than it looks, and I zip it halfway up. Hannah and Roxy would probably die if they saw me in it — Jess D. definitely would — it totally does not go with anything that I've bought with Roxy. All the rest of my hoodies are solid colored, except my pink CAPE COD hoodie, which Roxy finds acceptable.

Anyway, wearing this totally goes against rule number three: Don't wear your Geek on your sleeve . . . or bag. Or folder (ahem, *Hugh*).

Penny comes in holding a severed arm. "Oooooh, nice," she says, stroking the interior fuzz where I rolled up my sleeve. "This is *cute*. Where'd you get it?"

"They sent it to me. What are you doing with that arm?"

"Busted prop," she says, like it's no big deal. I guess if you work with stuff like that all day it isn't — but it's weird when it's on your kitchen counter. Back to the hoodie. "You may as well give it to me because you're not going to wear it."

I wrap my arms around myself. "No way. Get your own."

"Suit yourself. But it'll be gathering dust in your closet by the end of the week. And that's when I'll swoop in and steal it."

Before school, I peek at the contest boards on the Nightshade website. Looks like OakheartsBlade is still in last place, although he solved it quicker this time. And HeroKiller has almost as many points as I do — he must have finished the second puzzle pretty close to the same time as me. I shiver, grateful that I got it done when I did.

And Penny's right—I don't wear the hoodie to school, but I don't leave it in my closet either. It's hidden under my pajamas in a drawer so she won't find it. Ha!

In science, Hugh is wearing his new merch: a T-shirt with THE WARRIOR AND THE MAGE printed on it, with symbols for Sir Oakheart and Lady Althena. Huh. Kind of cool. Nirmal joins us—his partner is absent—and I spot him checking out Hugh's shirt too.

"Did you listen to the game the other night, Sarah Anne?" Hugh asks.

I did, and the Sox totally blew it against the Rays in the eighth. "My mom was shouting at the radio!"

We go back and forth about the game for a minute, then Nirmal says, "Hey, Hugh, that's not the shirt you got the other day, is it?"

"My brother won it and gave it to me for helping him out."

Wait—what? That's against the rules!

"He nearly got hit by a car from walking into traffic the other night, trying to solve the challenge," Hugh explains. "I kept yelling at him from the sidewalk."

Oh. Maybe that's okay.

We don't have much to do since Mr. O'Malley isn't letting us light stuff on fire during class time. We have to come back during his free period or do it at home.

They keep talking about the contest.

"Psst! Sarah Anne!"

Roxy waves at me from across the room. Mr. O'Malley is huddled at another table, working with a group, back to me.

"He doesn't get how Sam keeps finishing stuff first," Hugh keeps going. I try to ignore Roxy's waves. She glares at me, and I finally cross the room to her.

"You're going to get me in trouble," I say, voice low. Jess D. is pretending to doodle in her notebook, but she's totally listening to us.

"*You're* not wearing your headband," Roxy says.

Is she serious?

"Sorry. I forgot." Jess D. sighs like I've forgotten my right foot. I ignore her. "What's up?" She didn't call me over here to give me crap about my headband, did she?

"*Some*one gave this to me to give to you," Rox says, a funny grin on her face. She slips a piece of folded notebook paper into my hand.

At first, I don't get it. Why would anyone give me a piece of notebook paper . . . ?

And then . . . Oh. *OH.*

"Open it!" Roxy looks like a cat ready to pounce. I feel like one that has a fur ball.

"Um . . ." I need to stall. I don't want to do this in front of them. It'd just be questions and whispers and things I don't want to talk about.

"*I'll* take it," Jess D. adds, like she's being funny, but she's not.

"Pack up in two minutes!" Mr. O'Malley calls.

"Go back to the Geek Squad! Quick," Roxy whispers. "And tell me what it says."

"Don't get us in trouble," Jess D. says to me.

I cross the room, the piece of paper feeling a lot heavier than it should in my hand. I slide it into the pocket of my jeans.

When I get back to my table, I don't take the note out. Hugh and Nirmal don't even look up from their conversation.

Do I open it now? Do I wait? I can feel Roxy's eyes boring into me. She's going to want to know what it says at the end of class. So will Jess D.

Ugh.

I stick my hand in my pocket and pull out the note.

Hugh nudges me.

"What?" The word comes out sharper than it should have.

"I said, did you bring the sour cream 'n' onion chips?"

"Oh. Yeah. I have them."

Hugh sighs and goes back to Nirmal. They go on about some video game, and I turn my back to Roxy and Jess D. The note is on my thigh, "Sarah Anne" written on it in messy boy handwriting.

My stomach clenches. *If I don't open it, I don't have to know what it says.*

The bell's about to ring.

I need to tell Roxy.

I unfold the note.

Sarah Anne, will you go to the dance with me?
　　　　　　　　　　　　—Tucker

I think I might throw up.

22

"What did it say? Let me see it!" Roxy is all over me like the lacrosse defender from Wilson Middle School. Jess D. hovers behind her, totally listening in.

"It's at the bottom of my backpack," I lie. "I tossed it in there when the bell rang."

It's in my pocket, and I pretty much want to flush it down the toilet.

My hands shake, my heart pounds, and I feel weird and jittery, like the time I drank a large Xpress-o-Bomb from the coffee place downtown. Some girls must feel this way when a boy asks them to a dance because they *want* to go with him.

I do not.

"When did you even get the note?" I ask. We head to the other side of the building. Roxy has Spanish next and I have language arts.

"Jerry gave it to me to give to you this morning." Jerry and Roxy have their language arts class together. I frown. How am I going to get out of this?

"Do we know that Tucker wrote it?" I ask, grabbing on to an idea. "I mean, it could have been anyone."

Roxy frowns at me. "Of *course* he wrote it. What do you think this is, a movie? You're gonna go with him, right?"

"'Cause if you don't, I will," Jess D. chimes in.

My throat is blocked and words won't come out. I can't answer Roxy.

"You *have* to go, Sarah Anne. He's so cool. And I bet if you go, Jerry will ask me. We'll have so much fun!"

I just want to go with my *best friend* and have fun. Why does Tucker have to be involved? I totally can't have Jess D. go with Tucker. Because even though I don't want to go with him, Roxy and I are a team: We're best friends. We dress alike. We're the best lacrosse players. And now . . . we should go to the dance with the boys together. And if Jess D. takes that spot at the dance, what other spots is she going to fill?

That realization stops me in my tracks. I know I'm right. I'm losing Roxy to Jess D.

We're outside Roxy's Spanish class, with only a minute or so before the bell rings. Hannah, headed into the classroom next door, sees us and comes over.

"You won't believe it—Tucker totally sent Sarah Anne a note asking her to the dance!" Jess D. starts telling Hannah everything, and my guts squirm. I can't listen to this again—or deal with Jess D.

"I'm gonna be late," I say, and turn to leave, heading to class.

"We'll finish this at lunch since you don't have *time* right now!"

Jess D. calls out. I glance over my shoulder at her. Is it my imagination, or is she giving me a death stare?

Lunchtime. I can't bear the idea of going to the caf and sitting with the group, analyzing every bit of the note and how I'm going to respond and what I'm going to do about it. Plus, Tucker will be there, tormenting poor Eloise. What if I have to talk to him? No. Way.

But my options are limited: The library is closed (AT A TRAINING. BACK TOMORROW. KEEP READING! reads the note taped to the door), and we're not allowed in the gym during lunch.

I duck down a hall, hoping to hide in a girls' bathroom until I can figure out what to do, and there's Hugh. He's got a grocery bag and an Avengers lunch box. Dork.

"Hey, Sarah Anne. I was going to try to find you. Want to go see if Mr. O'Malley will let us work on our project?"

Best. Dork. Ever.

"Let's go!" I say. I'll deal with Roxy and Jess D. later.

Mr. O'Malley sets us up with the Bunsen burner and the other equipment we need. After a few warnings about safety and not burning the school down, he sits at his desk with a sandwich and quizzes to grade, leaving us to do the experiment.

Although I'm still freaked out by the note, being with Hugh is a lot less stressful than sitting with Hannah, Jess D., and Roxy. They'd be asking all kinds of questions about what Tucker said, what I'm going to say, and how I'm going to say it. Hugh just wants to know what kind of potato chip we should start with.

"Plain?" I suggest. "That way we have a basis for comparison, and we can see if flavoring and stuff affects the energy level."

Hugh agrees. We open the bag of chips and munch and burn stuff. They make a weird smell as they heat up.

"So . . . what else do you like, besides sports?" Hugh asks me.

"Besides sports?" I repeat the question like I don't understand what he's talking about.

"Yeah, you know — these games people play . . . ?"

I scowl at him. "Plenty of stuff. I like—" I almost say the Realm, but I catch myself. And then I pause again, because what else can I tell him that I'm into?

He waits.

"I like . . . movies," I say lamely. "What about you?"

"Nightshade stuff, obviously. *Star Wars.* My parents got me into that."

"Mine are way into it too," I offer. A chip goes up in flames and we drop it in the sink, laughing.

"So, uh, how's your brother?" I ask. I may as well take the opportunity to find out more about who he is.

Hugh stuffs chips in his mouth.

"He's okay," he says, mouth full, flecks of chip landing on the lab table. I try to ignore the grossness. "Why?"

"You said he almost got hit by a car or something . . . ?"

"Oh. That." He nods. "He's fine. It was just for that contest thing that he's in. Idiot didn't look up when he walked into the street. But he really wouldn't have gotten hit — the guy saw him and honked the horn." Hugh shrugs and writes down info from our chip.

I open the bag of salt 'n' vinegar and pass him a few.

"How's the contest?"

"Okay. I didn't think you were into that stuff."

"Just making conversation," I answer.

"They sent him some stuff," Hugh says, "for being in second place. He got this T-shirt."

"Why are you wearing it?"

Hugh grins at me. "Because he owes me for saving his butt. More than once."

I laugh. "Nice."

It's easy hanging out with Hugh. Even though I can't talk to him about the Realm, I don't worry as much about saying the right thing all the time. It's like I can breathe a little.

We torch a few more chips, and Mr. O'Malley tells us to pack up so he can get ready for his next class.

Hugh clips the chip bags and I wipe the crumbs off the table. With each swipe, the stress of my situation comes back. Once I leave here, I'm going to have to deal with Roxy, Jess D., and Hannah.

"What's wrong?" Hugh says.

"Nothing," I mutter. He keeps looking at me out of the corner of his eye, though, as I cram my notes into my backpack. And suddenly, I'm tired of pretending. Even if Hugh is not who Roxy or Hannah or I would normally hang out with, he's a lot easier to talk to.

"My friends are mad at me. Kind of," I say. "It's about a note."

"Oh," he says. Our workspace is clean. He slides his backpack on and we wave to Mr. O'Malley on our way out.

"Did you write the note?"

"No." We cross the hall.

"Is it about them?"

"No."

"Then it seems kind of weird that they're mad at you about it."

Huh. I guess it does. I don't know what to say without going into all the details, so I give him a half nod, half shrug.

Hugh heads his way (advanced math) and I go mine (French). I feel a little bit better until I see Hannah's ponytail bobbing down the hall a few people in front of me.

Then the pit in my stomach gets bigger. Forget Hannah, *Roxy* is headed straight for me.

I don't want to deal with her.

I *can't* deal with her right now.

Dodging some kids fumbling with their lockers, I duck into the nearest classroom. It's a language arts room. The teacher, one who I've never had, looks up. The warning bell rings.

"Sorry," I mumble. I pretend to search for something in my bag, zipping and unzipping pockets, my back to the doorway, head down, hoping that Roxy didn't see me and won't come after me.

Kids come into the room for class. In a second, it'll be really obvious that I don't belong here.

I sling my backpack over my shoulder and go back into the hall. Roxy is nowhere to be seen.

I jog from the language arts classroom to my French class, not looking at anyone on the way.

My stomach settles and I feel as though I've escaped dealing with Roxy and Hannah. I'm almost at the classroom. As I get to the door, someone grabs my backpack.

I don't want to turn around.

It's Roxy.

"Hey," I say, taking every bit of energy I have to sound perky and "fine."

She scowls at me. "You didn't come to lunch."

"Forgot that I had to do Science Showcase stuff," I say, hoping she'll believe me. "I was in Mr. O'Malley's room."

"With King Dork?" she says.

"Yeah," I say. "King Dork." I feel sort of bad, but it's also true. "You're going to be late." Roxy has math this period, and it's two halls over. She gives me a smirk like I'm acting like her mother or something.

"Bonjour, mademoiselle!" Mme. Mohr says. "Qui est t'amie?"

"Bonjour," I mumble. "Elle s'appelle Roxy."

"Roxy est dans une autre classe, n'est-ce pas?"

"Oui," I say.

"Au revoir, Roxy!" Madame calls.

"Au revoir, Roxy," I repeat, emotionless. *"Go."*

"You need to answer him," she whispers. "He was looking for you at lunch."

"Okay," I say, trying to get her out of the room. "Go!"

"Really?" she asks.

"Yes!" I say. *Why won't she leave?*

"Great! I'll tell him!" My stomach flips and my mouth drops open. *She tricked me!* Another bait and switch.

Roxy gives me a huge grin, but before I can grab her and tell her not to say anything to Tucker, she's gone.

Shaking, I take my seat and apologize to Madame. In response, she calls me up to the board to conjugate irregular verbs for the class.

Je suis. I am.

Tu es. You are.

Il/Elle/On est. He/she/it is.

I am angry.

You are a jerk.

It is a mess.

MOST FANTASTIC
FAN CHALLENGE
PHASE 2

23

I don't expect the next challenge so soon, but I open my email at my locker at last period and there it is:

Salutations, Adventurer!

It is time for your next challenge. We are moving to the next phase of the contest, and this time you will be assigned points for both speed *and* creativity.

Our messenger has delivered you a token from the Realm. Your next challenge: Photograph yourself and your token with as many people as possible in a four-hour window between Thursday and Sunday. You may choose the time, and you must submit your photos to the address below.

There was more — the hashtags to use, rules about getting permission (if you didn't have it, you couldn't post it to the public contest site but could still turn it in for points), etc. etc.

But none of that matters. What matters: *I have to wear the hoodie in public!*

My palms sweat just thinking about it. Rule number three is Don't wear your Geek on your sleeve. I never, ever wear any Nightshade gear in public. To tell the truth, it took me four months to wear the T-shirt that I have to *bed* — I kept it hidden in my drawer for the longest time. And do I even have to say that I never wear it at a sleepover?

If Roxy and Jess D. got worked up about me not wearing my coordinating headband, the hoodie would blow their minds.

Also, how is this even a *challenge*?! Taking pictures with people does not have anything to do with being a Fantastic Fan. Should I drop out of the contest and go to the dance with Tucker and be done with it?

That thought makes my stomach clench. It'd be miserable and awkward and weird with Tucker at the dance. This is my way out of that.

I picture Jess D. going with him, instead. They deserve each other.

But if I don't go with him, I may lose Roxy. I ignore the thought. One problem at a time.

I slam the locker and lean against it, hoping that no one can read the panic I'm feeling on my face.

Without thinking, I head down the hall that I always do. The hall where I always meet Roxy. At least she's alone.

"Don't be mad at me," she says. We head toward the doors. She adjusts her orange headband. "I haven't told him anything yet."

"Don't tell him anything at *all*," I warn her. "That's not cool."

"Come on, Sarah Anne. We'll have so much fun! Everyone will be looking at us, dancing with the two cutest boys in the school." I hadn't actually thought of *dancing* with him. . . . Oh no. I push the thought away.

"Is that what matters to you? That people will be looking at us?" I ask, genuinely curious.

Roxy stops and turns to me. "It's not that they'll be looking," she says slowly. "It's that we'll be like them. People will want to be like us."

I cannot think of one person who I'd like to be like less than Tucker.

I manage to get through the rest of the conversation, but feel gross about it the entire time. Roxy promises not to say anything to Tucker without my permission. Figuring out what I'm going to say to him is my next step.

At home, there's an old sheet spread across the kitchen table, and on top of that are all kinds of tubes and brushes and makeup. Wyatt's sitting in one of the chairs while Penny leans over him.

"Stop wiggling," she commands.

"It tickles!" Wyatt giggles as the brush goes across his forehead. He squirms in the chair.

Half his face is painted to look like a skull. She even painted over his lips to create the illusion of teeth in a jaw. Every bone is outlined and socket shadowed. Blood runs from his eye socket and from between his teeth.

"Whoa," I say. "That's so gross. It's amazing."

"Thanks." It comes out sounding like *hanks* because she has a makeup brush clamped between her front teeth. She takes the brush out. "It's part of my final project for class."

Penny's studying theater in college. She wants to be a makeup artist or set designer. She has the weirdest homework ever.

"Is the blood part of it?"

"There's *blood*?" Wyatt yells. "You told me there wouldn't be blood, Penny!"

Penny shoots me a dirty look. "It's fine, Wyatt. Sarah Anne knows you don't like blood. She's just messing with you."

Did I know that he doesn't like blood? I can't remember.

Now Wyatt wants to see his face and Penny mouths, "I will get you for this." She keeps saying that there's no blood on his face and quickly uses her brushes for the finishing touches.

"I need to take a picture of this for my project, Sarah Anne," Penny says, eyes on Wyatt. "I want you to take some while I'm working on it." Her tone really means, *You have no choice since you messed this whole thing up.*

I grab Penny's phone and take some shots: a close-up of her applying the makeup to his face, ones from a little farther away, and, when Penny steps back, one of the finished product.

Wyatt looks super creepy—one side of his face is totally cute brother Wyatt, the other side seriously looks like it has no skin or muscle. Penny is pretty much a genius.

Once I'm done with the pictures, she leans back over him.

"One more second, buddy," she says. With a few quick dabs, dashes, and swipes, the blood is gone and he's just a half skull.

"Voila!" she says, and hands him the hand mirror that's on the table. He grins. Well, one side of his face does, anyway.

"Wait till Noah and Bobby see this!" he yells, and races out of the house to show his friends.

Penny fills a cup with dish soap and water and drops her brushes in there. Then she gathers up the makeup and tubes. I help.

"How's the contest going?" she asks.

"I'm killing it," I say honestly, "but I'm afraid of the next challenge."

"Why would you be afraid?" She swishes the brushes and takes them out of the cup.

"You know that hoodie that you love?"

She nods.

"I have to wear it to school. Or somewhere. And take selfies with people while I'm wearing it."

It's obvious that she's fighting a smile. "Really?"

Annoyance floods through me. "You think it's funny, don't you? People will tease me! It's not even a real challenge. Just some stupid advertising thing." My voice kind of breaks at the end. This could go bad. *Really* bad.

"Sorry, Sarah Anne," Penny says. And, to give her credit, she actually does look sympathetic. "But part of this is about marketing. They want people to go see the movie, and the contest has them excited. Maybe it's not as bad as you think. Maybe it's time you own it."

131

"Easy for you to say," I mumble. People love Penny because she's Penny: amazing with makeup, artsy, and creative. *That is so not me*, I think.

Penny taps on the lid of her makeup toolbox. "Actually, I have an idea. . . ."

24

"We can totally do it!" Penny's eyes sparkle and she's so hot on this idea, she's basically glowing. "C'mon, Sarah Anne! It'll be awesome."

"I don't know. . . ."

Her big idea: painting my face with her theater makeup for the photo session. She thinks she can turn me into a creature from the Realm and no one will recognize me.

I am not so sure about that.

"Look. I can use a prosthetic nose, change your forehead. . . ." She pulls these weird rubbery pieces out of her toolbox and waggles them in front of me. "No one will recognize you. Honest. We'll even hide your hair under a bald cap or wig."

"Like the year we were vampires for Halloween?" I grab one of those easy-to-peel tiny oranges out of a bag on the counter and stab it with a fingernail.

"Not like that," Penny says, a sulky tone to her voice. I was in third grade and she was in ninth. Let's just say I ended up looking less like a vampire and more like one of those scary clowns who terrorize small children. Penny is still sensitive over it. "You saw what I did to Wyatt!"

She *is* pretty amazing. And has moved far past her vampire-makeup days. I pop the last section of orange in my mouth, sucking the juice out of it before chewing.

"If you really think you can do it. . . ."

She grins at me. "Peel me one of those things and let me show you my stuff."

Thirty minutes and four oranges later, Penny clicks through the *Mausoleum of Monsters* movie photo gallery.

"This one," she says, pointing at a wood sprite.

"Too lumpy," I say. The wood bark looks complicated.

Images of a cyclops, a blu bear, and a wraith flip by.

"No.

"No.

"No."

Then she gets to the ice dragon. We both suck in air.

They really are beautiful. Scales of blue and silver and white shimmer in the photo. The creature has short horns of blue crystal and lizard-like eyes. They can fly, of course, and their breath freezes instead of flaming. Everyone loves the ice dragons.

And suddenly, I want to be one *so bad*.

"Can you?" I ask, in barely a whisper.

"Maybe . . ." Penny begins.

"Do it," I say. *Anyone* would want their picture taken with an ice dragon.

"It's going to take time to figure out. When do you have to do the thing?"

"By Sunday." I can't take my eyes off the picture.

Somewhere, deep down, I know that I am not really going to look like the picture.

And somewhere else, I know that this is a terrible idea, going out in public dressed like a dragon.

But another part of me, the part that is drawn to those crystal horns, beautiful scales, and unnaturally green eyes, doesn't really care.

25

It's Friday, and Roxy's found me. She's standing in front of my locker, eyes narrowed and brows crunched up. I left the house thirty minutes early this morning, hoping I could get my books and hide out in the science room until homeroom, but nope. She must've had her mom drop her off.

"You're early," she says, arms crossed and frowning. There's no way I can get in for my one locker visit of the day until she's ready to move. I sigh and stand there.

"I have to work on French," I lie, knowing that the language lab is open early on Friday mornings. "We have a test."

Roxy still doesn't move.

"You're wearing your hair wrong. Again."

She'd sent out the text to the team last night: twin French braids. But in my rush to get out this morning I just did one braid down the back.

"I planned on fixing it when I got here." These rules are getting old, I want to add, but don't. It's a standoff.

"I've been waiting, but I'm done. You're talking to Tucker," she says, her words flat as a pancake. I can't tell if she's actually mad at me, or just really, really annoyed. I guess it's the same thing, isn't it? But I'm annoyed at *her* too, for messing with me.

"You almost tricked me into saying yes!" I say. "I told you I didn't want to go with him. That's a terrible thing to do."

Roxy shrugs. "Maybe. But we've already been over this. Say yes and we'll have fun together. Don't be lame, Sarah Anne."

"I'm not lame. I'm mad. And I need to go study," I say. She cocks her head and smirks at me.

"Hike up your big-girl shorts and let's go talk to your date," she says. She drapes an arm around my shoulder and steers me, forcefully, toward the gym hall where Tucker has his locker. I'm so surprised, I just follow along.

"You're going to go with Tucker, I'm going to go with Jerry, and it will be fun," she says to me through gritted teeth. Her mouth isn't even moving. Even so, I can smell the garlic cream cheese she had on her bagel.

What do I say? What do I say? What do I say? goes through my head on repeat.

We stop in front of Tucker's locker. Thankfully, he isn't here. Roxy keeps her arm around me, but tightens it a little, like she's afraid I'm going to run away if she lets me go.

She's not wrong.

It's getting closer to first bell, and the hall fills up.

"Has Jerry even asked you?" I say, trying to break the never-ending panic cycle in my brain.

Roxy shakes her head. "He's waiting for you to say yes to Tucker."

Great.

Then, from behind us, "Hey."

We turn, a weird, two-armed, four-legged beast, and there's Jerry.

"Where's Tucker?" Roxy says. It comes out kind of harsh, and she winces right after she says it.

"Sick," Jerry answers. He's wearing a Patriots jersey and a red baseball hat. "You're, uh, in my way."

Roxy ignores him. "Sick, as in he's not coming to school?"

Inside, I'm cheering. I've never been so happy for diseases in my life.

"Yeah, he's wrecked," Jerry says. "You want me to give him a message?"

He looks at me pointedly, like I should know what he means. I do, but I pretend that I don't.

"We just wanted—"

"To see if you are taking anyone to the dance!" I blurt, cutting Roxy off—and throwing her under the bus. She can kill me later, it's fine.

Jerry and Roxy have matching openmouthed stares. Roxy snaps her mouth closed first, but then opens it again.

"Ugghhh," Jerry gurgles. He closes his mouth. "Uh, no. Not yet." He drops his eyes to the sticky floor like there's something totally fascinating there.

I nudge Roxy. Hard. She glares at me. If she were a giant blu bear, my limbs would be scattered all over this hallway.

"Roxy doesn't either," I say, faking bravery.

There's a moment, after I say the words, when the three of us all hold our breath. It's like the minute when a leaning Jenga block tower hangs on, hangs on . . . crashes.

Jerry keeps staring at the floor. He mumbles something, but I can't hear him.

"Huh?" I say.

"I said, 'I'll go with you, Rox,'" Jerry repeats.

"Oh!" Roxy says, finding her voice. The bell rings, and, like we were all waiting for a reason, we take off for class.

I'm dead. But it's all worth it.

Bap! A palm shoves the small of my back, not too hard, but hard enough to cause me to lurch forward in the lunch line, knocking me into Taryn. . . . Somebody, who nearly spills her soup. I apologize and then turn around to Roxy.

"Dork," Jess D. says snidely from behind Roxy. I try not to let them see how flustered I am.

"Why would you even *do* that?" Roxy says. But Roxy's not talking about Taryn.

I pay for the bag of chips I've grabbed, and we head for our table.

I am ready for this.

"It was a favor—just like the 'favor' you did for me, carrying that note from Tucker. Now you're going."

Roxy flops into her seat and tosses the protein bar she bought onto the table.

"You tricked me into that."

"Feels terrible, doesn't it?" I point out. "But you got what you wanted."

She pauses for a minute, considering. "Fair. Now, about you and Tucker . . ."

"There is no 'me and Tucker,'" I snap. I'm tired of this. "He's kind of a jerk, or haven't you noticed? He's not *nice*." I rip into my bag of chips with too much force, splitting it and causing sour cream 'n' onion to rain onto the table.

"It doesn't matter if he's *nice*," Jess D. says, joining the table. "It matters that he's Tucker and he wants to go with *you*." She slides her tray with a salad right on top of my chips, which crunch under it. I glare at her.

Hannah shrugs and twists her ring so the two little green jewels face out. "You can't eat them once they've hit the table, anyway. That's just gross."

For some reason, Hannah's words make something in me snap. I'm angry that they don't seem to hear—or care about—my reasons for not wanting to go with Tucker, and it's a hot, reckless, out of control anger.

"*Fine*. Tell Jerry to tell Tucker that I'll go with him." I can't believe the words are out of my mouth.

"Are you sure?" Hannah asks.

"I'm sure," I snap. I feel sick.

"Think of how amazing it will be," Jess D. says. "You're so *lucky*."

A pile of frustration the size of the Mountain of Shame rises in me. I'm so over Roxy's constant rules about popularity and coolness. It's exhausting. I am not lucky. I am making a mistake and I know it.

There's nothing I can say, so I take a huge bite of my sandwich and turn away from them, surveying the caf.

Eloise is in her usual spot, the corner by the door to the gym. She's alone today, no Tucker hanging all over her, and her other geeky friend is either still in the lunch line or absent. There's an open book next to her, and she reads while eating. Her face, which is usually so pink and sweaty, is normal colored, and she seems pretty . . . relaxed. And happy. Like she doesn't mind being alone.

I guess, considering what happens nearly every lunch period, she probably *is* happier by herself.

Roxy elbows me in the ribs. "Hey!" she says loudly.

I scowl at her.

"We are talking about the dance," Hannah informs me. "And what Roxy is going to wear."

I tune in and try to pay attention as they discuss what mall stores they want to hit this weekend to find Roxy—and me—the best dresses for the dance.

"Mama can drive us," Hannah says, checking her phone under the table. Then she looks at Jess D. "You know, *the blond one*. We can have lunch there and shop after."

Jess D. flushes, and under the table I nudge Hannah's leg. I grin at her.

Roxy sets up a time and they make a plan. I nod and agree in all the right places, grateful that the storm has blown over but still feeling uneasy.

After I've tossed my garbage and am on the way out I realize why: Tomorrow morning I'm supposed to become an ice dragon.

26

"I've got it all planned out," Penny says as she lines up her tools on the kitchen table. It's too early on Saturday morning. Mom and Dad have taken Wyatt to T-ball at the park so we can work in peace. The old sheet is out again, and the brushes and sponges and paint palettes, plus the prosthetic rubbery pieces, make it look like a spooky operating room. I shudder and wrap my arms around myself.

"Go wash your face and pull your hair back," Penny instructs. When I don't move fast enough, she turns to me. "Do you want a ton of zits? Because that's what this stuff will do if I put it on skin that isn't clean."

"I'm going! I'm going!" I trudge to the bathroom, way more worried than excited. I know Penny's going to do an amazing job on my makeup, but I had to lie to Roxy, Jess D., and Hannah and tell them that I had to watch Wyatt this morning and that I'd meet them after lunch. They are going to be in the mall at the same time as me!! What if they see me?

For a second, I think I might throw up instead of washing up.

Breathe, Sarah Anne. Breathe.

I breathe. What would Lady Althena do?

I do what I have to to ensure the protection of the Realm, her voice responds in my head.

"I don't think the Linden Mall is as important as the Realm," I mutter out loud. I wash and dry my face, patting it like Penny taught me, instead of rubbing it, and clomp back downstairs.

Giving her the biggest, cheesiest smile I can, I thump into one of the kitchen chairs. "There. All cleeeeeeaaaaan."

"Good," she says. She's brought the desk lamp from Dad's office to the table, and she turns it on and shines it straight at me. I wince, and she angles it a little differently. The light's hot on my skin. Then she takes out a pot of some thick white cream, dips two fingers in, and smears it all over my face. It's cold.

"Yikes!" I pull away from her.

"Don't be a baby. It's just a moisturizing base."

She holds the underside of my chin with one hand, uses the brushes with the other. Her face is close to mine — really close — but she's so focused on what she's doing, it's almost like she doesn't see me. Her hair is pulled back tight, and she even has a cloth headband on to keep it away from her face — and my makeup.

Penny's kind of a mystery to me. She's seven years older than I am, so she was basically out of the house when I was still in elementary school. She's always been nice to me and Wyatt — when she got her license she would take us to the stupid kid movies we

144

wanted to see—and when she went to college she asked me to take care of Mr. Muffin, this giant, pink stuffed bunny that one of her boyfriends had given her. But we don't have that sister-bond type of relationship that you see in movies or memes where we hang out and share secrets. Sometimes it's like she's a friendly babysitter who used to live here.

"Close your eyes," she instructs. I obey. A cool, sticky slime is smeared across my forehead. Then she presses something on top of it—one of the prosthetic pieces, I guess. It feels like one of those stretchy toys that you get as an arcade prize—the ones that stick to a wall or window?—only this one is big and heavy and covering my eyebrows.

"Will I rip my eyebrows out when I take this off?" Roxy recently started tweezing hers, and although I have been thinking about it, this probably isn't the way I want to start.

"No, you won't rip your eyebrows off," she says in the voice she's going to use to boss around famous actors one day. "You'll take it off with the right cream and do it properly and you'll be fine. Now stop talking and let me glue."

27

"Are you done yet?" It's been *three hours*. My butt is numb, my face feels heavy and masklike, and I hate MK Nightshade and everything that has to do with the Realm.

"Almo-ost," Penny says, drawing the word out like she's singing. She dabs at my cheek with a tiny brush for the 9,235th time, then puts the brush down. She places her hands in the small of her back and straightens. Her hair frizzes out from around her headband. She scrunches her forehead and looks at me like she's studying a piece of art, tilting her head from side to side. Then she licks her thumb and wipes at something above my right eye.

"You're done," she says. "Let me shoot it for my portfolio, and then you can look."

While she gets her good camera, I imagine what I look like, but I can't stop worrying that it's a total failure. What if I look like me, only blue?

My life will be over.

Penny returns and takes several shots from all directions. I pose when she tells me to, but after what seems like a few dozen *turn this way* and *act like you breathe icicles from your face* requests, I get annoyed.

"Let me see," I say. "This is torture!"

She huffs out her breath. "Fine. Go look."

I bolt from the chair and race down the hall to the nearest bathroom. I don't want to use the handheld mirror. I need to see the final product all at once.

My heart pounds. I close my eyes, send up a wish and a prayer, and flick on the lights. Open my eyes. Gasp.

At first, I can't take it all in. My eyes only see it in pieces:

    - Two crooked, ice-blue horns

    - Light-blue scales at the hairline that darken to midnight at the chin

    - A flared-nostril snout that somehow is an optical illusion on my own nose

    - Delicate whorls in violet and midnight around my eyes

    - A glittering, built-up brow bone that flares to the side

I'm not me at all.

I'm an ice dragon.

Penny comes down the hall.

"You are a genius!" I screech. Not only will no one recognize me—*everyone* is going to want their picture taken with me. I am going to own this round, same as I did the first two. I want to throw myself at her in a super-giant hug, but I'm afraid of breaking my horns.

"You like it?" Her eyes glint mischievously.

"Like it? *I love it!*" My voice is at top volume. I bounce on my toes.

"Worth the time sitting in the chair?"

"Totally worth the time sitting in the chair." I'd pretty much sit until my butt melded with the wood to get this effect.

"Get ready. I'll drop you off."

I bound upstairs to grab my hoodie and tug on the dragon-scale leggings mom ordered online to complete my costume.

This is going to be amazing.

28

The nerves hit as we pull into a parking spot at the mall.

"You're *sure* no one will recognize me?" I ask for the thousandth time.

Penny flips the sun visor down and points to the blue scales and funky brows in my reflection.

"Do you really think anyone will look at that and think, *Ohmygod! Sarah Anne is in there?*"

"Okay, okay," I grumble. "You're right." I take a deep breath and close my eyes, hoping the fairies flitting around my stomach settle down.

Self-possession is the key to besting one's foes, Lady Althena whispers. She's right, I'm sure she is. But I feel like my foes could best me right now.

"You're good. Seriously," Penny says. She gives my hand a squeeze and presses a small bottle into my palm. "Just remember to take a break every hour or so and spritz some of this at the edges of the prosthetics. Otherwise they'll dry out and fall off. And here's the remover." Another bottle, accompanied by a bag of cotton makeup-remover pads. I stuff both in the plain black backpack that I borrowed from Wyatt. It also holds the permission forms that I need people to fill out, some water, and a change of clothes for when I meet Roxy, Jess D., and Hannah.

"Thank you," I say, riding a wave of gratitude for my sister. "I wish you could come with me."

"I'll be around," she says. "I have to get some stuff for the play, so I'll pop by and see how you're doing."

"But don't act like you know me," I say quickly.

Penny rolls her eyes. "No problem, weirdo. Ready?"

I gulp, nod.

She opens her door and, after two more breaths and a mental reminder that I *really* want to win this contest, I open mine too.

The stares start as we cross the parking lot. Little kids point and shout, and grown-ups pause, stare, and then keep going. At first, I want to fidget and hide.

Why did Penny park so far from the door?

We get closer to the entrance and Penny leans over, whispering in my ear. "You're a *character*. You're *acting*. Have fun with it." And then, before I can respond, she lengthens her stride and is in front of me like we don't even know each other. I'm on my own.

This is what you wanted, I remind myself.

The automatic doors whoosh open, and I'm inside.

If I thought the stares and the pointing in the parking lot were bad, this is ten times worse. People actually freeze.

I double-check to make sure that I'm actually wearing clothes.

And then, from up ahead a little voice shrieks, "Mommy! Look! A dragon!"

I spot her: blond ponytail and a pink-and-purple T-shirt. Her eyes are as big and round as a cartoon character's, and her hands clasp together under her chin like she's so excited that she doesn't even realize they're there. Something about her makes me think of Wyatt, and how he nearly exploded with delight when Mom and Dad took him to meet the guy who drove his favorite monster truck.

Without thinking, I wave at her and toss my head like I imagine an ice dragon would. She squeals and comes running right at me. I stop—conveniently in front of one of those digital kiosk things outside FanWear—and wait for her.

When she reaches me, she throws on the brakes, and her mouth drops open. She looks up at my face, and for a second I think she might cry.

But she beams.

"Mommy!" She turns. Her alarmed-looking mother is still racing over to us, like I'm a real dragon who will whisk her kid off to the Cave of the Wretched and the Lost. "Mommy! Can you take my picture?"

"Is—is that okay with the, uhhh . . . ?"

I nod. "Of course!" I crouch down, and the little girl leans into me. Careful not to mess my makeup, I make sure to keep my face away from her hair. Mom snaps the picture, and before they take off I dig a permission form out of my backpack.

"This is for a contest?" The mom gestures to the form.

"Yeah," I say.

"I hope you win!" She signs her part of the form and tears off the section that lists the contest hashtags. "I'll totally submit this."

"Thank you!" I call. They leave, and as I watch them go I become aware of the circle of people that has formed around us. Lots of shoppers must've stopped to watch me with the little girl.

"Can I be next?" The quiet voice comes from my left. I turn.

It's Eloise. My whole body goes cold, then there's a rush of warmth. I nod.

She hands her phone to her friend, the one who sometimes sits with her in the caf, and stands beside me.

"You look awesome," she says.

Tears spring to my eyes. I don't know why, but I know one thing: I am not going to be seen with Tucker at that dance.

"Thanks," I murmur. Photo done, Eloise steps away. I hand her the form, she signs it, and she's gone.

"Can I get my picture taken next?" A kid in a green Celtics cap calls to me.

"Yeah!"

He comes over, and this time it's a selfie.

"Rad makeup," he says, heading back to his friends.

This is gonna be a breeze.

29

An hour and a half later, it's feeling less breezy and more like work. There's been a steady stream of people who want to take selfies, touch my horns ("please don't"), and ask if I'm an ice dragon from the Realm. I'm hot and thirsty and I need to pee.

Now I know how Santa feels.

But Santa has elves, and a FEEDING THE REINDEER—COME BACK IN FIFTEEN MINUTES! sign. And he gets paid for his time.

A grandmother-aged woman comes over, phone outstretched. I go through my list ("contest . . . picture . . . social media . . .") and then show her how to use a hashtag. She giggles like someone my age when we take the picture and then gleefully shows her shopping buddy her new skills.

The next person approaches.

I'm kind of afraid to leave the crowd, because what if they all disappear when I'm in the bathroom?

A bead of sweat springs out on my forehead, and inside, I panic.

What if the makeup runs?

I want to wipe it, but I don't dare. Which is worse: me wiping and smudging or it running down my face and smudging?

The second I start thinking that way, I sweat more.

"Cheese!" A green-haired teenager snaps our picture. I'm more worried than fierce.

I check the notifications on my phone: 105 hashtag mentions.

One more, I decide. *One more and then I'm going to the bathroom to get my act together. I don't care if nobody is here when I come out.*

A guy with a long dark ponytail and a bunch of dangling earrings, wearing a FanWear store employee T-shirt, comes up to me. He tosses his ponytail over his shoulder.

"Pic?"

"Sure!" I rattle off the contest info and he leans in next to me, holding up his phone.

Just before he clicks the icon to take the picture, he tosses his ponytail again.

Some hair sticks to my eyebrow, and before I can get a word out, he says, "Thanks!" and walks away.

There's the smallest of tugs, and the silicone brow that Penny glued on comes loose.

I want to put my finger up there to stop it from falling off, but I'm afraid to do so without a mirror to guide me. Instead, I hold my hand across my forehead, like I'm a sailor searching for land.

"Be right back!" I bellow, far more loudly than I should. The crowd seems startled but moves out and lets me through.

The bathrooms are on the other side of the mall, so I speed walk and ignore the pointing and staring and questions ("Can

I have a picture?" "Where are you from?" "Are you practicing for Halloween?"). The restroom sign is up ahead, and exiting the Sparkle & Shine accessories store right underneath it are Roxy and Jess D.

I stop short and my whole body goes ice cold. I am legit afraid that I'm going to pee my pants from shock.

They can't see me like this. They can't see me like this. They can't see me like this. Theycan'tseemelikethis.

Halt this nonsense! Lady Althena's voice roars over my brain babble. *Adventurers do not quail in the face of the enemy! Forge on!*

I'm still in makeup. There's no way they can recognize me.

I take a breath, then keep going, hand still in front of my brows. Jess D. and Roxy stand in front of the store window, tapping at their phones. Why are they here so early? Where's Hannah? I will myself not to look at them, even when their heads lift to watch me pass. My heart slams, hard. *Don't look. Don't look.*

"What is *that*?" Jess D. giggles.

Don'tlookdon'tlook.

The restrooms are right in front of me. I hit the door and push inside.

Made it.

Thankfully, the bathroom is empty. After I pee, I assess the damage: The brow flap that Penny glued on has definitely come loose, and some of the painted-on scales around my forehead have smudged from the sweat.

It's not as bad as I thought — I expected that I'd be seeing blue streaks and my regular face—but it definitely doesn't look as good as when I left the house.

And now part of my face could fall off.

I remember the spray bottle that Penny gave me and dig it out of my bag. I was supposed to use it once an hour. Guess that is a hard-and-fast rule. I spritz the spot as best I can and try to press the piece back in place without totally ruining the makeup, but my fingers turn blue and it totally does not match the other eyebrow now. I don't know what to do.

The bathroom door swings open, and it's Jess D. and Roxy.

"Whoa, Dragon Princess!" Jess D. says. "What are you doing here?"

I can't answer. They'll recognize my voice.

Adventurers do not quail, I remind myself.

Adrenaline zips through my body and I want to run out of here, but they stand between me and the door. Here comes the sweat again.

I'm going to look like a Smurf, not a dragon.

I shrug.

"You don't know? What do you mean? Are you lost?" Jess D. needles.

I shake my head. Roxy passes me and heads into a stall.

"Your makeup is beautiful," she says as she closes the door.

Jess D. crosses her arms. "What are you supposed to be? I mean, I get that you're a dragon, but is it a certain kind of dragon?"

I just want to get out of here. I point to where a watch would be if I wore one, and then point to the door.

"Oh, am I keeping you? So sorry," Jess says. She steps to the side. She's not sorry.

I'm about to bolt from the bathroom when she says, "Wait! I get it now! You're from the MK Nightshade series. You're an ice dragon!"

I nod, reaching for the door handle.

"Ugh, so many people loved that when I was, like, eight," she says.

Her words pierce through my dragon scales and land in my guts. If she realizes it's me under here, I'm doomed.

Roxy flushes and comes out of the stall.

"Harsh, Jess," she says. She turns to me. "My best friend used to be into all that stuff too. She's outgrown it and all, but you do you."

Can you simultaneously want to hug and smack someone? 'Cause that's how I feel right now.

I bang through the door and go back into the mall. Only two more hours to go.

30

When I get back to my spot, there's no one there. I have to start over, only I don't look as good, and I'm honestly afraid no one will come.

After a few heart-pounding minutes, one kid stops, then another. Soon the crowd returns.

"Can I be next?" The familiar voice goes right through me: Hannah. Also early.

Mouth dry, I nod. She steps forward and digs her phone out for a selfie.

"You look really beautiful," she says. I don't dare smile. Can she hear my heart pounding?

She holds up her phone and we snap the selfie. I hand her the paper. She signs the form and waves. "Good luck!"

I am a sweating mess. If I were a real ice dragon, I would've melted by now.

. . .

After another hour and a half, my horns droop. My brows flap. And I am so sick of selfies I never want to see another phone in my life.

On the plus side, I stopped counting when I got to 130 tags. Now there are way more than that, so I better win this thing.

My phone's screen is crammed with texts: Evidently Jess D. was able to get a ride to the mall earlier than expected, so she and Roxy came early—and nearly caused me to have a heart attack. Then they looped Hannah in. There are also a bunch of texts asking where I am and when I am going to meet them. I have about thirty more minutes to stand here, but I'm suddenly nervous about being MIA all this time. Adding a few more pictures doesn't seem like that big a deal.

I take one with a little boy carrying a princess doll, and that's when I decide that it's over. I text my sister.

Penny comes up to me when I'm trudging to the bathroom.

"Whoa," she says.

"I'm done."

"Yeah you are."

She checks my makeup critically. "It held up okay," she says. "But I can tell you didn't spritz."

"I didn't exactly have time," I reply.

Standing at the sinks, I let her peel off the prosthetics and toss them in the garbage can. Although I'm kind of sad to see them go—the horns, especially—my face feels lighter without them. Next, we attack the blue paint.

Every time the bathroom door opens, I jump. "Chill," Penny says, swiping one of the cotton pads across my forehead. It joins the mountain of blue in the trash can. Although the makeup comes off easily, my skin has a funny bluish tinge to it.

"Easy for you to say." She doesn't have to worry about her friends seeing her like this. Her friends are actually into this stuff and think it's fun.

For a second, I wish my friends did too. It'd be cool to have people to share it with. Like Hugh.

She wipes, I wipe.

About four million cotton pads later, she pronounces me clear.

The mirror is not kind: My hair's a wreck in the front from the damp cotton at my hairline, there are dark circles under my eyes, and the cute yellow top I threw on under my hoodie is rumpled, like I wore it to bed.

I unzip the hoodie and pass it to Penny, who greedily throws it on and heads back into the mall with the warning to meet her at the entrance where we parked in two hours or she'll leave me behind. I redo my braid as quickly as possible, wishing I'd brought more than lip gloss in my—

Oh no.

I have the black backpack instead of my usual blue string bag. The girls are totally going to notice . . . *and they saw ice-dragon me carry it into the bathroom!* I want to crawl under the sink and stay here.

You spilled coffee on yours before you left, Lady Althena whispers in my head. *And many travelers carry black satchels.*

160

'Tis no bother. Grateful that they drink coffee and have good advice in the Realm, I take a breath, then whip out my phone and text them.

ME: I'm here! Meet you in front of Swag Shoppe?

I don't wait for the bubbles to appear to show that they're writing me back. I slip out of the bathroom, toss the bag over my shoulder, and head back into the mall.

'Tis no bother, I remind myself. *I'm part ice dragon, part Adventurer. And now: part secret agent.*

31

"Nice bag."

Of course it's the first thing out of Jess D.'s mouth.

"Wyatt knocked a full mug of coffee over on my other one. I had to take his." Lady Althena's lie rolls off my tongue easily, and my heart stays at a normal speed. I can do this.

"Are you feeling okay? You look a little . . . green," Roxy says. Her mouth is pulled into a tight line, concerned for me.

"Must be the light." I shrug. "And yellow isn't really my color."

"Not hardly," Jess D. responds. I roll my eyes at her.

"We've been here forever," Roxy says. "Well, Jess and I have."

"Yeah, I saw your texts when I got home from Wyatt's T-ball game." The lies keep coming.

"Where do you want to go?" Hannah asks.

I have a gift card that I want to spend, so the girls help me pick out two new shirts at one of our favorite stores. One shirt's shimmery blue and one's violet with silver trim.

Moving another shirt on the rack reveals a tee that reads SWORD + GUTS = LADY. Part of me wants it *so bad*.

"That's powerful," Hannah says. I can't tell if she's being honest or mocking me. She's got a dark-green sweater in one hand—it matches her "palette"—and sips from a water bottle in the other. I nod. Jess D. snorts and crosses to the other side of the store.

"Right?" I cover the tee again.

Roxy turns. "How's this?"

She holds a maroon tank printed with small gold dots in front of her.

"That color is amazing against your skin," I tell her.

Hannah nods, then squints. "Are they Golden Snitches?" she asks. We take a closer look at the tank and spot the wings printed faintly in gray.

"Bummer. I really like the dots." Roxy goes to put it back.

"They're totally hard to see," I point out. "You could get away with it."

Roxy's head whips around. "No way," she says. "That's not my jam."

Meanwhile, Hannah's found a shirt patterned to look like a python.

"These would go great with that!" I hold up a pair of gold dangly earrings beaded in similar colors to the shirt.

"Ugh. What are you *thinking*?" Hannah says. "You know I never wear gold."

Actually, I hadn't paid that much attention to her accessories choices, so whatever. I put the earrings back and think about the tee again. I'd happily swap out one of the other shirts for it.

What am I thinking?!

"Come look at *this*!" Jess D. squeals from another rack. Roxy trots off to see.

"Hey, you've got something on your neck," Hannah says to me in a low voice.

"My neck?"

She points to a spot below her left ear, toward the back of her neck.

"There."

I tilt one of the mirrors at the jewelry counter, and the girl behind the register scowls at me. Ignoring her, I tilt my head far to the right and peer into the mirror.

A blue streak runs from my hairline almost to my jaw. How could Penny have missed it?! My heart thuds and I try to wipe it away, but without the remover it won't come off—it just smears some more.

"Weird," I mutter. I can't let Roxy see it.

"Did you get your picture taken with the ice dragon too?" Hannah asks. I whip my head around quickly to look at her.

"Um, oh yeah! That's what it must be from. I saw it on the way in. You too?"

She nods. "It might stain your shirt. Maybe go to the bathroom after here?"

We get in line to pay, and I make sure I stand so Jess D. and

Rox can't see my left. Roxy keeps giving me strange looks, but I pretend like I don't see them.

Once we're back in the mall I rush to the bathroom. Of course they follow me. For a second, I don't know how I'm going to get the paint off with them standing there. Then I remember: The handicapped stall has a low sink and mirror in it. I duck in there.

"That's only for the disabled," Jess D. calls.

"Thanks, Mom!" I respond, opening the backpack.

Thankfully there are a few cotton pads left in there. I scrape at my skin with the pads and get the last of the blue off, then contort my head and neck in the mirror, trying to see if there's more that I missed.

"Everything okay?" Hannah asks when I finally come out. "Did you forget to flush?"

"I hate it when people do that," Jess D. says.

I hadn't even peed. I run back into the stall and flush the plain water, then make a big deal about washing my hands.

"All set, Mom?" I say sarcastically. Sweat runs down my back, and the skin on my neck prickles. I just want to go home.

"What time are you meeting Penny?" Roxy asks.

I check the time on my phone. I still have an hour.

I may not make it that long.

Longest. Afternoon. Ever. We spent the hour looking at dresses for the dance, but I didn't even try anything on. By the time I got to Penny, I was exhausted and stressed and just wanted to go to sleep. An ice dragon and Adventurer I may be, but a secret agent — not so much.

32

When we get home, Mom and Dad grill me on the day.

"How was it?"

"Did you get a lot of pictures?"

"Was anyone weird?"

Their questions come one after the other, leaving me no time to answer or think.

"Good. Yes. No," I say. Penny shows them the shots of my face before my hours-long photo shoot.

"Whoa," Dad says.

Seeing it again does make me ridiculously excited. Penny's pretty much going to win an Oscar someday.

"I can't imagine you not winning this round," Mom says. "I'd want my picture taken with you, and I have no idea what the ice dragons are!"

Their excitement gives me a boost, and before I hop in the shower I check the leaderboard—unchanged since the contest runs through tomorrow—and quickly scan my social media feed.

SAM's account has over two hundred tags, mentions, and notifications! Score!

I check HeroKiller's: So far, he has just over one hundred.

And OakheartsBlade has none, meaning he either isn't having any luck or hasn't started the challenge.

I click on one of the tags in HeroKiller's feed: He's the kid named Chris from the panel, the one in the hoodie with the bad mustache/patchy beard combo. In most of the shots he submitted, he's with high school kids. Not many of them are selfies — he must have had someone take the pictures for him. A bunch are in uniform . . . the soccer team, maybe? And the background looks like the high school. Interesting. He must've hung out after school yesterday and gotten some kids at the end of the day. He's not wearing a hoodie, though — looks like Nightshade, Ink, sent him a T-shirt. It's hard to see what's printed on it, but it's black — the same color as the one Hugh was wearing. In most of the photos, Chris is making a goofy face, posing and hamming it up for the camera like a normal kid. For a moment, I almost like him.

And then I remember how jerky he was to me on the panel, and I'm back to hoping he loses.

So that means OakheartsBlade is Ethan, then. The one who wore the BLOOD, GUTS, AND GLORY T-shirt. The one who hasn't submitted his photos yet.

And one of these two guys is Hugh's brother.

33

By Sunday night, it's official. Well, at least according to what I see online: Ethan also got around one hundred photos and tags. I've blown them both out of the water.

The premiere and trip to California are mine.

And *that* means no dance for me! Double reason to be excited.

And-and: all of it while still (mostly) keeping to my geek girl rules. *No one knows.* Even though the mall was super stressful, it was worth it.

If I weren't in my room, I'd take a total victory lap right now.

I scroll through some of my tagged images, reading the comments:

ALTHENAFAN32: Yo Sam, dope makeup!

CREATURTEACHR: Ice Dragon FTW!

ILUVBLUEBARE: Ice dragons r lame u should of ben blue bare

You should learn how to spell.

> **MYSHADENITESHADE:** Is this photoshopped?
> Amazing
> **NUGROOVE52:** You should win
> **HELLOPHO74:** Crazy #icebeatsfire
> **WENDYMCME:** Dude how long did that take?

And there are so many more. Aside from one or two complaining about my choice, people seem really into it. I keep scrolling.

I totally owe Penny.

Honestly, there was no way I could've gone out in public in that hoodie without her, and no way I would have gotten all those people to pose with me.

After a bunch more nice comments, I spot one that makes my hands go numb:

> Don't the rules say you can't have help? U didn't do this
> on ur own.

I hadn't even thought of that stupid rule applying to the makeup. I mean, I would never have asked for help answering the questions or solving the riddles. And it's not like Penny came to the mall with me and pointed people in my direction or anything. I did all the photos on my own, she just helped with the makeup.

It should be totally fine.

Right?

I toss my phone on the bed and pick up my lacrosse bag. Even though the sun is starting to go down, I tug on a sweatshirt — *not* the Nightshade hoodie! — and head downstairs to go outside.

"Where are you going?" Mom asks as I pass her at the table.

"Practicing," I answer. I don't stop, just call out, "I'll be in in a bit," and bang out the back door.

Outside, the mid-April air makes me feel a little better. I take a deep breath, unzip my bag, grab my stick, and toss the ball against the trampoline that's leaned up vertically against the bottom of the deck. It bounces, and I catch it in the pocket.

Toss.

Bounce.

Catch.

Toss.

Bounce.

Catch.

Soon the rhythm of the ball and catch takes over and I stop thinking about the contest, stop worrying about the makeup, and stop stressing over the dance.

Toss.

Bounce.

Catch.

It's just me, the stick, and the ball, until the sun goes down and it's too hard to see.

34

I don't see the email until the next day after practice. Coach Vaughn started making us leave our phones in the locker room—says they're "too much of a risk" to have on the sidelines, but honestly I think she's sick of the constant buzzing and beeping from alerts—so it's not until I fish my stuff out of the locker that I notice it.

From: organizers@nightshadeink.com
Subject: Photo Challenge

After peering around to see who is paying attention to me—no one, since Roxy is in Coach's office and the other girls are getting their bags together—I open the message.

Congratulations, Adventurer SAM! You accumulated the largest number of photos and social media tags for this portion of the challenge. However, due to claims that you received assistance during your challenge, we will not be publicly announcing the scores for this round yet. At your convenience, please call Paul at the number below so we can discuss this matter.

My heart hits the floor and my knees wobble. I lean against the lockers behind me and take a deep breath. Close my eyes.

Why is this happening. Why?

I just want to keep my fandom hidden, win the prize, go to the premiere, and go back to my normal life. Why is that so hard?

"You okay?" Roxy's voice startles me. My eyes fly open and I nearly drop my phone.

"Yeah. Fine." I stuff the phone in a pocket of my bag and smile at her. "Everything go okay with Coach?" I ask, trying to change the subject.

Roxy was trying to get permission to run track as well as play lacrosse—the seasons overlap. She grabs her stick bag and backpack and we head for the door.

"Yeah, she says I can do it if I keep my grades up and don't miss any games."

I make a noise of agreement, my brain already back on the email. It's not until Roxy calls my name that I realize she's no longer beside me.

She's about halfway down the hall, arms crossed, eyebrows raised. At the end, near the water fountain, Jess D. waits for us.

"Wha—?"

Roxy stomps toward me.

"Listen. What. Is. The. Deal?" She gives each word its own capital letter.

"I don't know what you mean," I say weakly. My heart pounds. I hadn't expected her to say anything, and I need my brain to come up with lies, excuses, *something*—for whatever it is she's going to ask.

"*You!*" Roxy flings her hands open like she's exasperated with me. "You're not yourself lately. You're always sneaking looks at your phone. You're not into the stuff that we usually do. You're not even trying to pretend to wear your hair the way the rest of us are. I saw the blue paint on your neck at the mall this weekend, but I didn't say anything because I was waiting for you to own it. Something is *up*, Sarah Anne." She ticks off every point on a finger.

I had no idea that she noticed.

"It's nothing," I try, still attempting to find the right words that will let me off the hook. "I just have . . . stuff . . . going on at home. We're good. Honest."

"Your family okay?"

"Totally." I nod for emphasis.

"Then you are hiding something. And that is not cool, Sarah Anne." She's gone from hands spread apart to arms crossed tight.

"I—it's embarrassing—I didn't want to tell you. . . ." I'm stalling.

Her eyes narrow. "Go on."

"At the mall this weekend, there was this person dressed up as an ice dragon. You know, from the Realm? They were doing it for some contest. Anyway, I took a selfie with them and that's how I got the paint on me, I guess."

Roxy rolls her eyes. "Of *course* you would do that. Come on. We're past that lame stuff. It's time to grow up, or everyone is going to think you're a loser." She turns, and I trail behind as she walks down the hall to meet Jess D.

Then I stop as Roxy keeps going, watching my life change when all I want to do is keep it the same.

35

Later, in my room, I pace around my phone, which sits in the middle of my bed like it's some kind of holy relic.

I am supposed to make a phone call.

I hate making phone calls.

Texting is better.

My parents tried to coach me when I came home, but their "advice" just got me more stressed out:

Dad: Be firm.

Mom: Listen carefully.

Dad: Ask questions.

Mom: State your case simply.

Dad: Be respectful.

Mom: Don't let them walk all over you.

Both of them: Do you want us to listen on speaker?

That's when I told them I'd just do it myself and ran up the stairs. UGH.

And now the phone, with its sparkly blue case that Roxy picked out, mocks me from the center of my bed, on the "sand-colored" quilt that Roxy told me would look "so sophisticated" with the black-and-white beach photos when we redid my room last year. *Sand colored* is another word for *beige*. I hate beige.

I also hate the phone. But I'm supposed to call "at [my] convenience." *What does that even mean?*

Right now, I feel like it'd be convenient for me to call sometime around the year 2045. I sigh. I pick up the phone. Put it back down. Pace some more.

I have homework that I need to do. Maybe I should knock out my math problems first?

Do they have business hours? What if I miss them and have to leave a message?

The only thing more awkward than making a phone call is leaving a message.

The phone sparkles from the bed. Taunting me.

I wish I could take it outside and toss it like a lacrosse ball.

Instead, I grab it and tap the highlighted number in the email before I think anymore.

It rings, and my mouth goes dry.

I didn't cheat.

"This is Paul."

I try to swallow, but I can't. Something between a wheeze and a choke comes out of me.

"Hello?" Paul says, his voice annoyed.

"Hi, it's Sarah Anne—uh, SAM. You, uh, wanted me to call you?" I'm out of things to say.

"Oh, hey there, Sammy," Paul says. "So, are you having a good time with the contest?"

Picking at the edge of the quilt on my bed, I nod, then answer. "Yeah, it's good."

"You're doing really well, Sam. Really well. And, um, I'm sorry that I have to ask this, but as you may know, it's come up that you may have received help with the last challenge?" It all comes out in one long sentence.

"The pictures? My sister helped me with my makeup and then I went to the mall. She dropped me off. I took the pictures myself."

Believe me believe me believe me.

There's silence. I chew on a hangnail.

Paul sighs. "Just the makeup?"

"Just the makeup."

"No help with getting people to take pictures with you?"

"No way. She was shopping the whole time and I didn't see her till she met me in the bathroom." UGH. Why did I say the part about the bathroom?! "To take the makeup off," I add lamely. The hangnail rips off with a needle of pain. My finger bleeds.

"It was pretty awesome," he says.

"Right? She's good."

I can almost hear him thinking.

"Look, Sam, what she did isn't technically against the rules, but you can kind of see it that way. The makeup helped you get the attention for the photos."

I don't say anything. My brain empties and my knees go weak.

He's going to disqualify me.

Sink onto the edge of the bed. Wait. Breathe.

"But the rules don't say that you can't wear costumes or anything. . . ." he says it out loud but like he's talking to himself. "So . . ."

I wait, every muscle tense. My shoulders have climbed to my earlobes.

"I guess it's okay. But if you decide to do something like that in the future, you need to run it by me first, okay?"

Relief rushes through me. My shoulders drop to where they belong.

"Yeah. Yeah, of course. Thanks, Paul."

And I end the call before he can change his mind.

36

It's all over the message boards. People are split into two camps: They're either psyched for me, or they hate me.

> **OATHBUILDR:** SAM cheated. No way they should let him stay in the contest!
> **GHOST23:** SAM's awesome. Double points for creativity!
> **BRO309:** Dude should be DQ'ed.

Reading them makes me feel kind of ill. On the one hand, it's not like they know it's me — most of them think I'm a boy, which is weird, because I'd think the shiny dragon-scale leggings would have given it away. In this case it could actually make me feel better. It's like reading about myself, but not. How does that even make sense?

But the negative comments make me feel gross — even though

they don't know me, they call me a dude, and they can't see my face. It makes it almost worse.

There are hundreds of comments on this thread—way more than any of the others. I scroll and scroll, and after a while I stop reading but keep scrolling, watching the words blur together on the screen.

A text comes through.

ROX: Lax tomorrow at Wilson. Ur mom's driving?

Oh no. I'd forgotten that we were scrimmaging against the other junior high team tomorrow, and I was supposed to ask my mom to do the carpool.

I race downstairs. Mom frowns when I ask her.

"What's my rule?"

"Thirty-six hours' notice," I mumble, shifting from foot to foot. "I'm sorry. It's been a crazy week." I don't add *If you were on the parent group text, you'd already know.*

Mom opted out of the group text for lacrosse parents last year, when a mom used the list to try to sell everyone this antiaging cream and diet plan with vitamins and protein shakes.

"I am fine with my wrinkles and like to *chew* my food!" she shouted at the phone one night, when fifteen pinging texts came in in a row.

So, yeah. I'm supposed to give her notice and keep her filled in.

She sighs and checks her calendar. "I can do it, although I have to move a conference call," she says, making me feel like I'm a burden.

I slink back to my room and send Roxy a thumbs-up emoji.

Hair back, she responds. Single braid. Don't forget.

We coordinate before games and scrimmages. Roxy usually picks and everyone agrees. She texts the team, and the responses start piling up on my phone.

Usually I chime in, but after reading all the messages on the message board, I'm done. I turn the phone on Do Not Disturb, put it facedown on my bed, lie back, and close my eyes.

I still have homework, and I should go out and practice, but for right now I'm happy with my photo challenge victory and grateful that Roxy still texted me first about the hair for tomorrow.

Things are okay.

Things are good.

Right?

37

Coach Vaughn calls us to a pre-scrimmage huddle. We drape our arms around one another and put our heads to the middle.

"What's more important than winning?" she calls.

"Playing hard!" we respond as loud as we can.

"Then let's play hard!" she shouts.

We break, and those of us heading out to the field go that way, while the rest of the team stays on the sidelines. Roxy and I fist-bump. I triple-checked the messages before the game and braided my hair exactly like I was supposed to.

The Wilson girls are in green and yellow. The girl I'm defending dangles her green mouth guard out of the side of her mouth, chomping on one side of it with her teeth. She grins at me. I smile back. Their team hairdo is side ponytails, and she flicks her long brown one over her shoulder.

"Guards in!" the ref calls, noticing. She stuffs it in her mouth, and her formerly friendly smile is now a witchy grimace. I hold my stick tighter.

The ball's in motion, and I'm running downfield, staying with the midfielder, when I hear a name being yelled from the sidelines. And not by Coach Vaughn.

They're so loud!

"Sam! Sam!" I turn my head. A bunch of older boys who I don't know hold Howard Hoffer Junior. High signs and are shouting for someone from the other side of the field. But we don't have a Sam on our team.

Creepy.

"Go, Sam!" they shout as I race toward the goal. Wilson is *fast*.

They keep shouting, and when I turn to cross the field and see the familiar high school soccer jerseys they're wearing, I realize who they are.

It's Chris.

From the contest.

He and his friends are yelling for me.

What the—? I nearly stop dead, but I remember that I am in game mode and need to keep going.

"Hey, Sam!" They jump up and down, clapping and hooting.

I want to die. How did they figure out where I —

You are known throughout the Realm, Lady Althena interrupts. *They herald your name.*

That "one to watch" newspaper article! Chris must have seen it.

Meanwhile, the girl I'm defending changes direction and, since I'm looking at the sidelines while I work all this out, I'm left in her dust. Scrambling, I speed up to try and catch her.

Roxy passes me. "What's your deal?" she yells.

183

"Sam! Hey! Great job!" the boys call.

My heart beats faster than it should, and I've lost my midfielder.

"Focus, Sarah Anne!" Coach Vaughn's voice cuts through the sideline chatter. Everyone else is on the far side of the field. I have no idea who has the ball.

The whistle blows and we go to the sideline for a time-out. I turn my back to the guys, who are thankfully on the Wilson sideline, and then immediately regret it. What are they doing over there?

"Sarah Anne, you're struggling today," Coach says. "Take a break. You're out for now."

Roxy shoots me a look.

My face burns, but Coach is right. I have no business being out there. I try to pay attention as she details strategy for the next play, then Roxy and the others head back out.

I can't watch the game, only Chris and the guys waving at me.

I want to run away, throw up, and hide. All at the same time. I can't take my eyes off the group of boys, who hang around across the field from me, calling my name and waving. Then they switch to yelling "SAM! SAM! SAM!" and jumping up and down.

"What's up with them?" Jess D. asks. She's always on the bench. I pretend that I don't hear her and force myself to look at the field.

Follow Roxy.

I look for her dark braid and the gold ribbon she tied at the end. She's at the far end, in front of the Wilson net, alone, about to shoot. She pulls her stick back, quick, and—

"SAM! SAM! SAM!" The boys dance now, doing every trendy dance move in the most awkward, not-smooth way possible. (Is there really *any* way to be smooth when doing trendy dance moves on the sidelines of a girls' lacrosse game with no music? Didn't think so.)

Even the girls on the bench with me stare.

"They are so weird." Jess D. giggles. "It's hilarious."

Not even a little bit.

Roxy jogs into my field of vision, frowning and fierce.

"What's wrong with you guys? Where was the Howl??"

The Hoffer Howl is what we do when we score. Oh, crud.

"Great job!" I say, tilting my head so I can keep one eye on the guys, who have gone suspiciously quiet.

She turns, trying to see what I'm staring at.

"Sarah Anne! You're in!" Coach tells me, saving me from dealing with Roxy.

For now.

I jog onto the field. The boys go crazy. Chomping so hard on my mouth guard that I'm afraid my teeth might go through it, I purposely turn my back on them and face the Wilson girls. The ref drops the ball, and there's a scrimmage.

"SAM! SAM! SAM!" The chant worms its way into my head, and I've lost the girl I'm defending. I scan the field for her ponytail. She's got the ball and is on the way to our net.

I take off.

"SAM!!" This time it's extra loud. Still running, I turn to look at them.

They've stretched out a long white piece of fabric.

It's got words on it.

They read: SAM: QUEEN OF THE REALM.

Oh. My—

I'm airborne.

Then . . .

BAM!

Not anymore.

38

My lungs aren't working. The fall knocked the wind out of me and left me with a face full of grass. I don't want to move. The ref blows the whistle, stopping the game. I feel, more than see, my teammates gather around me. I close my eyes.

"Sarah Anne, are you okay?"

Did they see the banner?

"Can you move?"

Will they know what it means?

"What happened?"

"Take a second and breathe." Coach Vaughn's by my side, her voice in my ear.

I nod into the grass. I could move, I just don't want to.

"Get the trainer!"

But I have to.

I open my eyes and turn my head. Lots of cleats.

"Give her space!" the ref snaps. The cleats move back.

I put my hands under my shoulders, push-up style, and climb to all fours. My body aches. I went down *hard*.

"Take it slow," Coach says. I wince and stand. My back twinges and my palms and knees burn. "Go in. You're getting looked at."

"I'm fine," I protest, but I'm saying that out of habit. Getting out of here is exactly what I want to do.

The trainer comes to the field and I let her put an arm around me. Roxy stands on the edge of the crowd, frowning and skeptical, as I limp across the grass.

The banner, and the boys, are gone.

I spend half the ride home reassuring my mom that I'm okay, and the other half avoiding Roxy's cocked eyebrow and skeptical expression. She sits in the back seat with Jess D. and Olga, saving her dark looks for when I turn to talk with them. I give up, and the three of them giggle and look at their phones for the rest of the ride.

Roxy knows something's up, and I am in for more hurt than that fall gave me if she finds out what's going on. I reminded my mom a million times not to mention the contest while we were in the car, and I really, really hope she remembers.

"What was up with those guys on the sidelines?" Roxy asks after we drop off Jess D. and Olga at Olga's house.

"I'll text you later!" Jess D. calls.

"Guys?" Mom's surprised, and this is Roxy's revenge for my lies. My insides loosen.

"Just some kids from another school," I say casually, willing my mom to stop paying attention. "They were messing around on the sideline, distracting the players."

"Distracting *you*," Roxy corrects. "Why were they calling you Sam?"

Mom hits the brakes at a stop sign a little too hard, and we all rock against our seat belts.

"They were calling *your* name?" Mom hasn't moved the car into the intersection. There's no one around, and we really should be moving by now.

Stop it, Mom. It's because of the contest.

I beam mental energy at her, willing her to read my mind.

Unfortunately, parental panic seems to have taken hold.

"What did they do to you? How do they know you? Did you meet them online?"

I am going to murder Roxy.

"You need to drive," I remind her. "I think one of them is the older brother of my *Science Showcase* partner." I emphasize *Science Showcase* as much as I can, because she knows the deal about Hugh's brother being in the contest.

"Oh. *Oh*," she catches on. The car rolls. Thank goodness. "He's a bit of a troublemaker, that kid," she goes on, much more cheerfully, making stuff up to cover for me.

Even though I'm grateful, can we not talk about this anymore?

"You really think that one is Hugh's brother?" Roxy pipes in. "What's the deal?"

Actually, I hadn't made the connection . . . but yeah. Chris is probably Hugh's brother. Since we live in the same town, it'd be easy for him to find me. The realization makes me feel unsteady, almost dizzy.

Trying to hide my confusion, I shrug and fiddle with the radio. The new Theo Christmas song comes on, and I crank the volume.

"OMG I love this song!" I cry, a little too excited, hoping Mom catches on.

"Me too!" Mom says, and in thanks I vow to give her a week's notice before I ever ask her to drive carpool again. She belts the lyrics as loud as she can, and soon we're all singing, drowning out Roxy's question.

Roxy joins in at the chorus. She has a good voice and can carry a tune better than me or Mom, so we actually sound halfway decent.

But no matter how loud we sing, worry gnaws at me.

How much longer can I keep this going?

39

Over the next week, I recommit to my normal life:

I don't check the leaderboard. To make sure I don't, I clear my browser cache and delete the bookmark.

(Please don't let there be any new assignments.)

I wear what I'm supposed to wear to school, practice, and at home — bye-bye, beautiful hoodie; hello, sparkle shirt, tights, and skirts.

I erase all thoughts of Chris at the lacrosse game.

I pay attention to Roxy and text her constantly after school about Jerry and the dance.

I giggle at all of Jess D.'s lame jokes.

(This is the hardest thing to do.)

And, most of all, I avoid Tucker. I am not going to go with him, but I don't want Jess D. to take my place.

And it works. Roxy seems normal, going with my explanation that whatever I've been doing at home is over.

Part of me worries that I'm missing something, but the other part of me doesn't care. Things right now are uncomplicated. Easy. What I'm used to. The Lady Althena in my head even goes quiet. Maybe she's napping. I also make the time to take Wyatt out for that smoothie I owe him.

We sit in Java 'n' Juice, him with a giant strawberry-banana-chocolate concoction and me with a mixed-berry blast. He's brought three of his monster trucks and has them lined up on the table.

"Dis one's Blue Wave. He has the biggest wheels. And dis is Spoke Snapper, he looks like a lobster. Dis one is Mighty Monster."

I grab the red one, make a mountain out of napkins, and drive over it making truck noises. "I will crush you!"

Wyatt giggles, and smoothie dribbles onto his chin. He wipes it with a napkin.

"You love these cars, huh?" I say.

"They're trucks," he says. "I do. They are big and drive over stuff." He's quiet for a few seconds. "And nothing tells them what to do. And they crush things."

His words hit me hard. The truck mows down more napkin mountains.

Roxy tells me how to do my hair and what to wear.

Jess D. tells me how to treat kids like Hugh.

They're *both* telling me to go to the dance with Tucker, because it'll make them look better.

This is getting old.

• • •

In science, Hugh and I gather the data for our Science Showcase project.

"What should we do to share our results?" Hugh asks, chewing on the eraser of his ice dragon pencil.

"I think we should show it in a bar graph," I answer, liking that he asked me first. At the beginning of this assignment, he would've just told me how we were presenting it. "They're easy to read, and people like getting info quickly."

He shrugs. "Sounds good to me."

"Everyone, remember that your Showcase presentations are due to me at the end of the day on Thursday," Mr. O'Malley calls from the front of the room. "This is our last in-class work day. Do the rest on your own time." There's a groan from the class.

"We have to do the presentation materials and the slides," I remind Hugh. "Can you meet at lunch?"

He shakes his head. "I have an orthodontist appointment tomorrow."

We toss around a few other times — free periods (don't line up), during after-school help time (I have lacrosse).

"Guess you should probably come to my house after practice tomorrow," Hugh says. "The Sox are playing at night, so you won't miss the game."

I do not want to go to Hugh's house. That would not be good.

"Uh, what about you come to mine?" I say.

"I have the stuff already," he points out. "It's kind of silly to lug everything to your house when all the equipment and data are already at mine."

He's right, but I don't want him to be. I rack my brain. How do I ask him if his brother will be there?

And then, it's like he hears me: "Oh, and my brother will be around. He can help us with the presentation part. He won the Science Showcase when he was in eighth grade, you know. And he totally owes me."

Of course.

Of course he did.

"Great," I say weakly. "Can't wait."

40

I stand outside Hugh's house, sweaty and smelling terrible, wishing I were anywhere else. Stupid Science Showcase. Stupid MK Nightshade universe. Stupid everything.

The intrepid Adventurer returns to face her fears. Lady Althena is back, and disdainful. I've disappointed her.

Well, *she* doesn't have to worry about being in her enemy's house. *She* can go jump in Prince Obsidian's volcano.

Mom hasn't driven away and I haven't knocked on the door. I take a breath, wipe my face on the sleeve of my sweatshirt, and bang on the door—harder than needed.

Loud barking—like, dangerous animal–sized barking—comes from the other side of the door.

I turn and wave at Mom—mostly to ensure that she drives away and I can't race for the car and throw myself in the front seat—and the door opens.

It's Hugh, holding on to what seems to be a real-life blu bear who is the source of the huge, booming barks.

"Hey," he shouts over the sound. "Berrick, sit!" he commands the beast. The fur mountain sits, stops barking, and cocks a head the size of a basketball at me.

"Is that . . . ?" I haven't moved.

"It's a dog," he says. "He's a mutt—we think he's sheepdog and something else—and super friendly. He might lick you to death."

"Something else . . . like a grizzly bear?" I ask, trying to joke and not show him that I'm terrified his dog will eat me.

Hugh grins. "More like the world's largest teddy bear."

I move to step in, and the beast jumps to his feet and barks some more.

Not gonna lie, I almost pee a little.

"He needs to sniff you first." Hugh wrestles with Berrick's collar. "Like this." He holds a closed fist in front of Berrick's face—*the perfect way for him to rip off my arm*, I think. "Your turn," Hugh insists. "Trust me," he adds when I pause.

I squeeze my hand into a fist, and—I can't help it—I close my eyes when I stick it in front of Mount Berrick.

There's a delicate sniffing, a gentle puff of air on my closed fingers, and then a rhythmic thumping.

"He likes you," Hugh says. I open my eyes. My limb is still attached, and the gray fur pile bangs his tail on the floor. His mouth is open, tongue hanging out.

"Is he . . . smiling?" I edge into the house, expecting Berrick to rip me to shreds, but instead he turns and follows me as I follow Hugh.

"Yeah. He does that." Hugh leads me through the house, into

the kitchen. Their kitchen is white and blue and not cluttered like ours. A big blue bowl of lemons and oranges sits in the center of the island. I can tell that no one is allowed to touch any of that fruit.

On the other side of the room is a table with Science Showcase stuff spread out on it. I plop my bag on an empty chair and pull another one out to sit on. It's weird being in Hugh's house — a boy's house — and it's also so *quiet*. Where is everyone?

"My parents are working," he says, like he knows what I'm thinking. "Mom's office is in the attic. She'll be down later."

All that's running through my head is: *Where's your brother where's your brother where's your brother?*

The back door opens, and there he is.

It's Hoodie Chris.

Wearing his stupid hoodie. His mustache and beard are gone, though.

He grins as he comes into the room.

"How's it going, Sam?"

Hugh laughs. "It's Sarah Anne, not Sam."

I am frozen, like this is a surprise. Like I hadn't known this was coming. Like I don't have a single comeback in my head.

(Okay, I don't. Why didn't I prepare for this?)

"Hey," I mumble. I keep my eyes on the tabletop, staring at a bag of smokin' bbq chips.

Out of the corner of my eye, I see Chris go to the fridge and open it. He comes out with some electric-blue sports drink in a bottle.

"How's that Science Showcase project coming, Hugh? Need some help?"

I say no at the same time that Hugh says yes.

Chris laughs.

"Sounds like you're having a *banner* day," he says, stressing the word. "Guess you better figure things out."

For some reason, those words make me mad. I mean, *I'm* the one beating *him*, right? Why does he get to be a jerk to me about it?

"While we do that, why don't you go study?" I toss at him. "Clearly you have some stuff to brush up on."

Hugh's head swivels back and forth between the two of us.

"I don't need to brush up on anything. I need people not to *cheat*."

"I'm not cheating!" The words are loud — okay, I'm yelling — and Chris smiles. He's gotten under my skin and that's what he wanted. A victory for him.

I fume.

"Uh, do you two know each other?" Hugh asks.

I don't answer. Chris just grins.

"Wha . . . wait . . ." Hugh looks from me to Chris again. "Sarah Anne, are you Sam? The kid in the contest?"

My face is hot and red and I hate everything.

"Oh, whoa," Hugh goes on. He leans against the tabletop and shakes his head. "I had no idea. You're *killing* it! Congratulations!"

Not what I expected. I glance up at him. Chris slurps his drink and scowls.

"The ice dragon makeup? That was incredible. How did you do that?"

"Yeah," Chris echoes. "How *did* you do that?"

There's a lump in my throat and I can't speak. I shrug and shake my head. "My sister is a theater major. She painted my face."

Hugh looks from me to his brother. "She is kicking your *butt*, Chris."

"She didn't look so good on the lacrosse field the other day," he sneers.

"That was low," I snap. "Totally against the rules."

"Oh, like getting help with your makeup?"

"Paul said that was okay. *You* just hate losing to a girl!" I'm standing now, and Chris and I are on either side of the kitchen island, basically shouting at each other.

"I'm not losing to anyone," Chris snarls. He stomps out of the room, footsteps pounding up a set of stairs that I can't see.

My heart's pounding too, and my face feels big and hot, like it does after I've been playing in a lacrosse game. I turn to Hugh.

"Secret's out," he says with a grin.

My life is pretty much over.

41

I hold my breath, waiting for what comes next. Afraid to look, I keep my eyes on the table.

"I think it's pretty cool," he says. "You must know a lot of stuff about the Realm to be so far ahead in the contest."

"Well, it's not that hard. Your brother knows nothing about the Realm," I tell the tabletop.

"Can't hear you."

I raise my hot face and don't look at him. "Your brother knows nothing about the Realm," I repeat. "It's why I'm wiping the floor with him."

And hey, it feels good to say it out loud, so I say it again. "I'm wiping the floor with him." I smile, and sneak a look at Hugh.

He grins at me. "You pretty much are. He needs a lot of help."

He asks me a couple of questions about the contest and MK Nightshade, and as I answer I have this weird, out-of-body experience thing.

I haven't talked to a real kid my age about MK Nightshade in *years*. And I kind of like it. I mean, I hang out online in the message boards, but I'm super careful, and who even knows if the people I'm talking with are kids or adults or creepers.

But this—this is even different than that. It's like we have a language, a shorthand.

"Prince Obsidian?" I ask.

Hugh rolls his eyes. "He's part magma monster. You know it."

"You think so too?" I squeal, I'm so excited.

"Rochlan the Brave?" Hugh throws it out there.

"Totally Lady Althena's brother!" We say it in unison.

We keep doing this back and forth as we work on our project, and I can feel myself relaxing—really being myself—for the first time in a long time, let alone since this whole thing started. I hadn't realized how afraid I was for so long.

Then, as we're talking, I realize something else. "You know way more than your brother about this stuff. Why aren't *you* in the contest?"

A cold wave comes off Hugh. "It's a long story," he says stiffly. And that's it.

It's such a reversal that I don't know what to say. But what I start to feel is that fear coming back, wrapping itself around my chest and tightening its grip again. Hugh knows everything—who I am, what I'm doing, *and* that I'm trying to beat his brother. I'm not safe.

"Please don't tell anyone about me," I blurt without thinking. I hear the desperation in my voice and I hate it.

Hugh cocks his head just like Berrick. "Tell anyone?"

"Yeah, like Nirmal or Roxy or . . . anyone. I don't want anyone to know I'm in the contest." My hands twist the hem of my shirt on their own. I stop them, and they immediately go to the edge of my shorts. Sliding into a chair at the end of the table, as far away from Hugh as I can get, I struggle to get control of myself.

"Why don't you want anyone to — Oh." Hugh cuts himself off as the realization creeps across his face. "No one knows you like the Realm. 'Cause it's not *cool*."

It's like he threw a bucket of cold water at my face. My whole body goes numb, and my brain stops working. I don't know how to respond to him.

Is there a response to him?

"Uh," I try, but I don't know where to go after that.

"I get it," he says, leaning over the table and shuffling our work. "I guess. After all, you're friends with Roxy and Jess D. and Hannah, and play lacrosse, and Tucker asked you to the dance. . . ."

How does he know about that?

He trails off, but it doesn't matter. It's like being stung by bees over and over. Shame floods me, and I drop my head to the table.

He turns away from me and pulls the Science Showcase stuff over to him.

"I think I'm done," he says.

He's not the only one.

42

Later, back at home, I can't stop worrying about Hugh. I mean, he *knows*. He knows *everything*. What if Roxy, Jess D., and Hannah find out? They'll totally tell Tucker.

Upside: I definitely won't have to worry about the dance anymore.

Downside: Jess D. will go with Tucker, Roxy will go with Jerry, and they will have a great time being friends forever without me.

My stomach hurts.

I curl up on my bed. The Science Showcase is next week, and the dance and the premiere are just two weeks after that. This is agony.

There's a knock at my door. I grunt, and Mom pokes her head in.

"You okay?"

"Yeah."

She comes in and sits at the edge of the bed. "What's wrong?"

"My stomach hurts," I say, grasping at the easiest explanation. *I am afraid my life is falling apart because of the stupid contest* is just too complicated.

She frowns and smooths my hair. "Can I get you anything?"

Witness protection?

"No thanks," I say, closing my eyes and sticking my face in the crook of my arm so I don't have to look at her and feel bad about lying.

She shifts on the bed, rocking the mattress.

"Do you want to talk about it?"

Do I? All the issues blow through my mind like leaves in a strong breeze: accidentally agreeing to go to the dance, getting wrapped up in the contest, Chris and his teammates unfurling the sign, and — the one that hurts the most, surprisingly — Hugh's face in his kitchen when I told him that I wanted to keep everything secret.

"It's just . . . hard right now," I say, eyes still closed, head still covered. It's easier to talk to darkness.

Mom's hand lands on my back, and she rubs circles there like she did to put me to sleep when I was little.

"I don't want anyone to find out about the contest, and it's hard to keep the secret."

Mom's hand pauses. "That's because some secrets aren't good to keep."

Those words don't make me feel better.

"What do you mean?" I snap, moving my arm and opening my eyes. It's hard to snap at someone with your eyes closed.

Mom's hand is back in her lap. "It's just . . . who you are, Sarah

Anne. Why do you have to hide it? Dad and I don't hide the fact that we're *Star Wars* fans."

"But you're old and people expect parents to be dorky," I point out. Mom squinches her eyebrows together at me.

"Maybe, but we also own who we are and what we like," she says. "And if you can't do that, you're denying who you really are. You're pretending to be someone else. And that won't last. Is any of this *you*?"

Sitting up, I scoot back to the head of the bed and cross my arms.

"It's only until the stupid contest is over."

Mom sighs and crosses her own arms.

"But at what cost?"

I want to pretend that I don't know what she means — but I see Hugh's hurt and imagine Rox drifting away, and my stomach muscles clench again. I know exactly what she's talking about.

"It'll be fine," I mumble.

Mom stands up, pecks me on the forehead, and turns to leave.

"I hope so," she says.

Me too.

43

There are helium balloons coming out of a locker halfway down the hall.

They aren't fun-looking balloons, or the streamers and posters we use to decorate someone's locker on their birthday or when their team wins a big game, just plain gray.

Kids point and giggle at them as they walk by. As they walk by my locker.

The balloons bump together lazily, and as one turns I see the badly-drawn crest of the Realm on it.

It's like I'm in a dream — I want to run, but my legs weigh a thousand pounds each and I'm finding it hard to move.

Roxy stands across from the bunch of balloons, arms folded. She turns her head toward me. I freeze.

My heart slams, and I need to get out of here, only I don't know where to go. I can't leave the balloons there — I still can't see what's on the others — but I really don't want to talk to Roxy.

Forcing myself, I keep going. Hannah stops next to Roxy.

There are five balloons decorated with black marker: one with the crest, one reads ADVENTURER, one has the URL of the leaderboard, one shows the *Sea of Serpents* creature.

And one has a terrible drawing of my SAM avatar from the contest. Of course.

Ignoring Rox and Hannah, I grab the ribbons that come out of the vents on the door of my locker and pull as hard as I can, with all the anger and fear that's in me.

There's a plastic-sounding *snap* on the other side of the door, and a tangle of gray ribbon comes out of the vent.

But now what to do with them? Popping them means more unwanted attention from the noise, and it's not like I can race through the halls, trailing them behind me to let them go outside. So I stand in the hall, the world's worst balloon salesperson, wishing they would lift me out of here.

Hannah is at my elbow.

"Gimme," she says. For a second, I wonder if she'll make a scene with them, draw even more attention to my nightmare, but she's not Jess D. She's not Tucker. She's not mean. I hand her the knot of ribbons, moist from my sweaty hand.

I pretend like I don't see the kids taking photos of them with their phones.

She winds them around her hand, bringing the balloons lower and lower, until they're below shoulder height. Then she takes them to the nearest garbage barrel. Roxy follows. One at a time, using their teeth, she and Roxy rip a hole in each balloon. Then they squeeze the helium out and drop their shriveled corpses in the trash.

Simultaneously grateful and horrified, I wait for them to finish.

The first bell rings as they cross the hall back toward me.

"Get your books," Rox says.

Numbly, I open my locker. Pieces of pink plastic—a handle that the balloons were tied to—litter the inside. There's no note, not that I'm surprised. It's not hard to figure out who did it.

But *how* is another story.

"So?" Hannah says.

"Thanks," I whisper. "Um, I gotta go."

Rox doesn't say anything else to me, but the angry expression on her face does it for her: There's a storm coming straight for me.

I can't focus in my morning classes. To avoid Roxy, I race to the bathroom when the bell rings and then get to my next class just before I can be marked tardy. But by the time I get to Mr. O'Malley's room, I'm as frayed as the end of a shoelace.

I plop into my chair. Roxy, by good luck, hasn't arrived yet.

But Hugh has.

And then it hits me: There's only one way Chris could get into my locker—he had to have a kid here at school do it.

And who could that be?

A fire monster blooms in me, and I turn around.

Hugh's at his table, talking with Nirmal. I send laser eyes in their direction.

I'm staring so hard, it doesn't even register that Rox has sat down next to me. Not until she says, "Not even a *thank-you*?"

Ice water quelches my hot anger and I suddenly remember that I'm supposed to be avoiding her.

"Thanks. Sorry," I say.

In front of the room, Mr. O'Malley gets the class started.

"You are a sneaky liar, Sarah Anne," Roxy whispers to me, "and you better tell me what is going on. That was all Nightshade stuff on those balloons, wasn't it?"

"It's nothing," I say as quietly as I can. Mr. O'Malley stops talking about acids and bases long enough to give us one of his "stop it now or I make a scene" looks.

I clamp my mouth closed so quickly that my teeth click together.

Roxy scribbles in the corner of her notebook and slides it closer to me:

What. Is. The. DEAL?

Nothing. I write on my own notebook.

She reads my response, frowns like she's thinking, and writes again:

What about the emails?

Huh? I make a row of question marks on my page.

She cocks her head at me, like an "oh, really?" gesture.

My guts twist.

"Ladies," Mr. O'Malley calls, "do you need some time to finish whatever conversation you're having? You can come up here and I can wait."

209

"Sorry," I mumble, face hot, at the same time that Rox says, "no."

For the rest of the period, I try really hard to concentrate on the demonstration Mr. O'Malley gives and the fact sheet he passes out. But all I can see are the questions that go with my situation:

Who put the balloons in my locker? Hugh?

If it wasn't him, then who else could it be?

What emails is Roxy talking about?

What does she know about the contest?

What's going to happen once kids see their friends' pictures, or get a chance to check the link on their phones?

Maybe this is the out that I've been looking for with Tucker.

The bell finally rings, and I push out of my chair to get to Hugh just as Roxy grabs my arm.

"Talk," she commands.

Hugh shoots a dark look at me as he bolts from the room.

A sharp pain hits my chest, and I almost can't breathe. Roxy shakes my arm a little. "Hey. Over here."

I can barely hear her, because now I know: Hugh put the balloons in my locker. He helped his brother sabotage me.

My heart splits like Lady Althena's when she was imprisoned in the turret.

44

Roxy doesn't let go of my arm until we're outside the classroom and standing against a wall. I'm boxed in.

I've been boxed in a lot lately.

"Spill."

"I don't know what you're talking about," I say, stalling for time. I can totally do that for the entire passing period, can't I? At lunch I can hide in the library or something.

She makes a face. "Start with the emails. The ones from the weekend?" Rox thumbs through her phone, holds the screen up to me.

TOTALLY READ THIS! shouts the subject line of one.

BEST. MOVIE. EVER. is another.

DON'T MISS THIS is a third.

"That's spam," I say. I look more closely at the address: sarah-anne231. "That's not even my account."

"It's all MK Nightshade stuff, and I know how much you *used*

211

to be into that," Roxy says. "Or am I using the wrong term here? I mean, those balloons were pretty obvious."

My mouth goes dry. "Those were . . . a joke or something," I manage to say.

"You have been hiding stuff and lying to me for *weeks*, Sarah Anne," Roxy says. The anger in her voice is clear. "This is not what friends do. At least, not people who *I* want to be friends with."

I don't know how to answer her or what to say. I have been lying, and I hate it. But it's not like I can tell her the truth now, when it's so close to being over.

"Everything will be back to normal soon," I promise. "Seriously."

Roxy shakes her head slowly. "You don't get it," she says. "It's not going to *be* normal. Not now. Maybe not ever again." She turns to leave, then turns back. "You know, you haven't been a good friend to me. We haven't talked in weeks. Jess D. knows more about my life right now than you do." She walks away.

I want to grab her, stop her, but what can I tell her? That she's got it wrong? That I'm trying to protect myself? She's mostly right: I haven't been a good friend to her. I *have* been wrapped up in my world. I chose to enter the contest thinking I could keep my secrets. I can't. And that's costing me more than I ever imagined.

So I watch her disappear into the crowd of kids heading to class before I head to language arts, feeling less like an Adventurer and more like a total jerk.

• • •

Jess D. smirks at me when I pass her in the hall later. "Nice balloons," she says. She wasn't even there. I don't acknowledge her at
all, just keep walking.

And while I'm focusing so hard on not looking at Jess D., I
nearly miss Hugh, who's trying to sneak past me.

"Hey!" I throw out an arm, stopping him.

"Hey!" He freezes and scowls.

"Why'd you do it? Why did you do that to me?" My hot anger
has melted and I feel like I'm going to cry. "I told you that I'm trying to keep everything a secret."

"I don't have to play by your rules," he snaps.

"But you play by your brother's?" I cross my arms.

He winces, and I stand there, fuming, while other kids
pass around us like we're islands in a river of backpacks and
sneakers.

"He made me, okay?"

"How could he *make* you? Did he march you to my locker like
you were going to be executed on the Slab of Sorrows?" I can't
even look at him.

"It's not like that," Hugh says in a low voice.

"Then what *is* it like, because I thought we were friends?" The
first bell rings, and I jump.

"Friends?!" Hugh, who up until this point had seemed like he
felt bad for what he'd done, steps back, eyes wide and mouth
open.

Uh-oh.

"You *lied* to me! And you and your friends act like me and my friends are total"—he struggles to find the right word—"*wastes*, because we're into our fandom. *The same one you're into.* You're a complete hypocrite, Sarah Anne! You're—you're two-faced."

Pink patches splotch his cheeks, and his jaw moves from side to side.

Shame creeps up through me, but I fight it. After all, *I* wasn't the person who broke his trust and put balloons in his locker.

You just ignored or made fun of him, Lady Althena whispers.

"I am not! I made it clear who I am and what I'm about," I say. "And you traded that info with your brother. What was in it for you?"

He looks away.

"Did you tell him about the lacrosse game too?"

"Lacrosse game?" I can't tell if he honestly doesn't know or is faking it.

"Yeah, your brother and his soccer buddies brought a banner to my lacrosse game."

Hugh shakes his head. "I had no idea. Chris didn't know that I knew you until you were in my kitchen. What happened?" He honestly seems concerned.

"They distracted me and I fell." That's all the info he's getting. Hugh shifts from foot to foot. The bell's going to ring soon, but I have one more question for him.

"Did he promise to take you to the premiere if he won?" Hugh flinches, and I know that's it.

I turn away from him.

"Sarah Anne," he says.

"I have to go to class," I mutter.

And even though I know that what he did was wrong, as I stomp down the hall a tiny part of me thinks he might be right.

45

At dinner, my parents glance at each other with the heavy expressions they only use when one of them is going to have to do something really uncomfortable with us—a yucky doctor's appointment, or delivering bad news.

It's me. I know it.

"I received a difficult phone call today," Mom says, clearly getting the smaller straw in their silent draw.

I don't say anything.

"Coach Vaughn is concerned about your performance in lacrosse lately. And your most recent progress reports had some . . . discouraging notes on them." She shifts in her chair, turning to my dad a little, to bring him into this. "*We* are thinking that maybe this contest has been a little more than you bargained for." She says that *we* extra firmly, so I know she and Dad aren't in 100 percent agreement. At least, they weren't at the beginning.

Dad gives me a weak nod.

This is going in a very bad direction. Clamping my mouth shut, I sit and wait. I'm going to make them say it.

"We think it may be time to consider dropping out of the contest."

The words land on the table like mini bombs, ticking off the seconds until they trigger my explosion.

I am not going to give anyone that satisfaction.

"No," I say simply. "I'm not going to quit now."

They exchange glances across the table again, then Dad taps in.

"Sarah Anne, your schoolwork is the most important thing. Then lacrosse. Those are in the real world. This contest—"

"This contest is real too," I point out. Inside, I am a mess of rage and disappointment, mixed in with all the recent friend drama. If this dam breaks, I won't be able to stop the flood.

"We don't want you to continue," Mom chimes in.

"Well, I'm not going to quit. Are you going to call and quit for me?" Crud. I know she doesn't like that tone. It comes off as a challenge, and she never backs down from one. *Stay in control*, I caution myself. *Stay. In. Control.*

"If we have to," Mom replies.

I push away from the table and grab my plate, and as I'm depositing it on the counter I hear Wyatt saying, "She didn't ask to be excused! Sarah Anne, you have to ask to be excused!"

I want to scream, but I don't. I keep going, up the stairs into my bedroom.

And when I hit my bed, I stick my head in a pillow.

And *that's* when I scream.

When I'm done, I roll over and let myself fall into the pit of blackness that I've been standing on the edge of all day.

What have I been doing all this for?

At first, it seemed like a good idea: win the prize, show how well I know the fandom, have fun. But it hasn't been fun for a while. It's been a stressful, annoying, hard thing. And for what? Even trying to keep it all secret, it's ruining my life. Everyone — my parents, Roxy, Hugh, Coach Vaughn — is mad at me.

I'd cry, but I'm not much of a crier.

Mom's words from the other day come back to me: *You're denying who you really are.*

And then I wonder: *Who am I, really?* The lacrosse star/popular kid with cool friends and a date with the popular boy to the dance? Or a total geek girl, into her fandom and science and . . . Hugh?

Into *Hugh*? Where did *that* come from?

The scary part: I don't know the answer. At all.

46

Turns out that pit of blackness is more of a pool: It's like swimming through tar to get through the day. Roxy's not talking to me. Hugh hands me a list of things to do to finish my part of our project for the Showcase, because he doesn't want to work together anymore. I can't say I blame him.

But the worst is at lacrosse. We have a game coming up on Saturday, and Coach tells me that she's not going to have me start. "Your head's not in it right now, Sarah Anne," she says. "And that's okay for you, but that's not fair to the team."

I'm pretty much not fair to anything.

Tucker's standing outside my math class when the period ends.

"Hey," he says. He tilts his head so his hair flops into his eyes in a way that's supposed to be cute but I think makes him look dumb.

"Hey."

"So, uh, I heard that you're not starting at the game this weekend?"

"Who told you that?" I've started walking to science. He keeps pace with me.

He shrugs. "Point is, that's not cool, Sarah Anne. We're going to the dance together."

"What does that have to do with the lacrosse game?" I'm so irritated I forget to be impressed by his very presence.

"Look. We're going to the dance 'cause I think you're cool. And playing second string isn't cool. So, can you fix that?"

Is he kidding me?

"Oh, sure," I say, sarcasm dripping like honey in a honeycomb. "I'll totally change Coach Vaughn's mind and get her to let me start this weekend."

"Okay, cool." Tucker actually looks relieved. He didn't get it. "I gotta go to social studies. See ya." And he takes off down the hall. A few girls nearby watch him with dopey looks on their faces. Ugh. *Really?!*

When I turn to walk into class, Hugh is standing there. He probably heard everything that Tucker said. I ignore him and sit at my table.

Roxy comes in next, and her eyes slide over me like I'm not here. She puts her stuff down right next to me, slides her chair as far away from me as possible at the two-person table, shifts in her seat so her back is to me, and promptly starts talking with Jess D. Message received.

Ms. O'Mara, the media specialist, comes in to talk with Mr. O'Malley. They go over to his desk, and everyone in the class keeps talking.

Everyone except me.

Maybe it is time to give up. Then I could let things go back to normal.

I mean, would it kill me to go to the dance with Tucker? So many other girls think he's amazing; no matter what else happened it wouldn't hurt my popularity.

But would you be true to yourself? Lady Althena chimes in.

I could go back to being friends with Jess D. and Roxy, if they'd have me.

And talking about things that don't really interest you and wandering about the mall like an aimless vagabond, Lady Althena says.

I ignore her.

I could focus on lacrosse again.

I could forget how fun it was talking with Hugh about the Realm, the Red Sox, and our project. How connected and relaxed I felt.

Lady Althena says nothing to that one. But I can picture her sitting with a smug smile on her face.

Nirmal, who'd been at the pencil sharpener, comes down the row. And Jess D. sticks her foot out and nudges her backpack into the aisle, just a little too far. Nirmal trips. He doesn't fall all the way, but does an exaggerated arm flail to keep his balance. Jess D. mouths "dork" and her tablemate giggles. Roxy may or may not join in, I don't want to know. It makes me feel sick and angry.

Adventure calls, my dear. Will you heed its clarion tone?

And, suddenly, I know: I sure as heck will.

HEEDING THE CALL

47

When I get home, I get to work:

Dig through my pajama drawer for the MY OTHER HORSE IS A CHARIOT tee.

Text Penny: I want my hoodie back. NOW.

PENNY: 😮 Check my closet.

It's there. I put it on, zip it halfway up. *My* choice.

Armored.

Tear down the beach-scene posters and the "sooo sophisticated" motivational quotes on my bedroom walls.

Ball up the "perfect with your aesthetic" beige comforter and stick it in the laundry.

The old posters are still tucked behind my desk, against the wall. My old comforter is in the linen closet. Musty, but I spray it with that laundry stuff, shake it a few times, and spread it out. This is what *I* choose.

Move the books from the bottom shelf to the top one. These are what *I* like.

Sir Oakheart and Lady Althena glare down from my walls in their fiercest fighting stances, swords raised.

The map of the Realm covers my bed.

My guides are on my shelf.

I'm wearing my armor.

Ready.

Let the war begin.

MOST FANTASTIC
FAN CHALLENGE
PHASE 3

48

Before the charge from redecorating wears off, and before I lose my nerve, I grab my phone and text Hugh.

> **ME:** I am a jerk, and an Adventurer of the Realm. Falling on my sword. Will you join my quest, or stay with the poseur?

I tap the SEND icon and fling the phone onto my bed. I don't want to stress over whether or not he sees it and is writing back.

Next, I log in to the contest site for the first time in days. There's been a new challenge issued—the final one. My body goes cold.

You strayed from your mission, Lady Althena whispers.

Chris and Ethan are way ahead of me in points on this one.

I launch the challenge.

Greetings, Adventurer! The journey has been long, but we near the end. This is the final challenge, the results of which will be combined with the others to determine the victor of the Realm.

An embedded video appears. I click the PLAY icon, and a clip from *A Sea of Serpents* begins. It's the scene where Saleed Oakheart, half sister of Sir Oakheart, declares her fealty to him and the Realm in the presence of the Council of Il. It's the scene that makes everyone cry, because Saleed knows that this allegiance means her death.

The video ends, and I'm feeling the feels like I do every time I see it.

The Adventurer message reappears.

As an Adventurer, like Saleed, you must declare your fealty to the Realm. Post a video, photo collage, or some other media that shares why you are a Fantastic Fan, and the inhabitants of the Realm will cast their votes for the Adventurer with whom they most identify.

Then there's a list of rules and regulations. The very first one states, "Participants may use costume or cosplay, but are prohibited from face makeup, masks, or any type of face shield."

Gotcha.

My heart hammers. I stand and pace around my room. Can I go public? Even though I was ready for Room Renovations 101, I am still not 100 percent sure that this is the right thing to do. It feels too soon.

But then again, what *is* the right thing to do? Pretend that this is not what I'm into, that this is not who I am? I'm done with that.

Supposedly.

I watch Ethan's and Chris's videos. They're pretty straightforward: wearing their Realm T-shirts, standing in front of boring backdrops, lots of "uhs" and "ums." They've each gotten a bunch of thumbs-up icons from viewers. But who knows if anyone actually watches them, or if they're just "liking" their posts. That thought actually makes me feel somewhat better.

And although I'm nervous about doing it, I start planning what I'm going to say.

An hour later, I've basically written my speech and have a good idea as to how I want it shot. I wish Roxy and I had taken TV production last year instead of theater, because I have no idea *how* to do what I want to. So frustrating.

Added to that: The challenge ends tomorrow, so I need to have the piece up tonight to ensure that someone will at least watch it. Nightshade, Ink, will send a blast to everyone when my video goes live.

There are lots of comments asking where my video is, because Chris's and Ethan's have been up for two days.

No time for fancy, then.

I open the camera app on the computer, stare at the screen, and hit RECORD before I can lose my nerve.

"Greetings, travelers," I begin, "you know me as SAM. And I always thought I was the biggest MK Nightshade fan, except . . ."

Ugh. Staring at myself on the screen, trying to remember the script and saying it out loud is awkward. I restart.

". . . you know me as SAM . . ." I flub a line.

I'm a mess. I decide I just need to get through the whole thing once with no recording. So that's what I do. I read my notes out loud, like Miss Vogel taught me to in theater class in sixth grade.

And I do it again.

By the third time through, it feels more natural. I'm even ad-libbing a few things. I can picture Lady Althena smiling and cheering me on.

I'm ready to record.

I open the app again, press the button, and go.

". . . I own my choices. I own my decisions. I own the Realm," I finish.

It comes out okay, I think. I don't mess up any lines, but if I go back and watch it I'm afraid I'll lose my nerve and start all over.

Now comes the hard part. I log in to my portal on the site and find the upload instructions. I read through them one more time, add the video, and pause, right over the PUBLISH button.

What am I doing?!

Winning, Lady Althena responds.

She's right. I click PUBLISH, watch the wheel spin, and, just like that, it's too late to do anything about it now.

Behind me, the phone on my bed buzzes. It's Hugh.

Absolution given, reads the text—it's the same phrase that Lady Althena uses to forgive Sir Oakheart in *A Mausoleum of Monsters.*

Another cloud of bubbles appears, and then his message: I humbly accept the invitation to be part of your party.

ME: Good. 'Cause my lying days are over

Charging forward, I text Roxy next:

ME: I've been a jerk. I'm sorry. I have stuff to tell you.
Can we talk?

This time, I bite my nails, stare at the phone, and wait for her to respond. I'm glad that Hugh and I are back on good terms, but Roxy has been my friend for a long, long time, and it's hard to imagine my world without her.

After an agonizingly long five minutes, the message changes from DELIVERED to READ, and bubbles appear.

ROX: Why should I care what you have to say?

Instead of writing back, I take a picture of my room and send it to her.

I'm making changes, I add underneath it.

ROX: 😮 Dad'll drop me off in an hour.

49

The slowest, most stressful hour of my life passes. While I wait for Roxy, I pace and straighten my stuff and have about a million second thoughts.

Dad knocks on my door.

"Hey—oh!" he says when he sees my room. "That kind of answers my question."

"Oh?" I'm trying to be cool, but this is the first time anyone has seen what it looks like now, and what if he laughs at me, and even though he's my dad and wouldn't do that he still totally could, and—

"I was doing laundry and wondering why your comforter was in the pile." He looks around again, more carefully and slowly this time. "Looks good. More like you." He winks and closes the door.

My heart, which had been pounding like it was going to explode, slows down.

Which is probably good, because when the doorbell rings I jump so high I could leap over a blu bear.

"I'll get it!" I wail, racing down the stairs. All the pent-up, anxious energy comes out in a burst of rocket fuel. Wyatt stands near the front door, mouth open as I tear down the hall. "I got it!"

"She's got *something*," he says to the Batman action figure in his hands. He steps aside as I throw myself at the doorknob.

It's not Roxy.

A terrified-looking delivery guy holding a white plastic envelope and a digital clipboard asks me to sign. His eyes are the size of softballs.

"Uh, sure," I say, trying to sound cool when we both know that I was the maniac on the other side of the door. My face flushes.

He hands me the envelope after I sign my name, then he turns to go back to his truck. Roxy's dad's car pulls in right behind it. She hops out.

I've spent all my manic energy on the delivery person, so all I can do is stand in the doorway, hold the package, and try not to go to pieces out of fear.

It's not easy.

Roxy wears her serious face—lips pursed, eyes narrowed. I give her dad a weak wave as he pulls away.

"Can't wait to hear what this is all about," she says, squeezing past me into the hall. Wyatt closes the door and holds Batman up to Roxy.

"She was running like a supervillain!" he tells her.

"Should we capture her? Call Commissioner Gordon?" she teases. She's always gotten along well with Wyatt. Everyone does.

"Uh, let's get a snack. I have to give this to my"—I hadn't even looked at who the thing was addressed to—"mom."

Roxy crosses her arms. "I don't need a snack. I need answers. Let's hand that over and play show-and-tell."

"I love show-and-tell!" Wyatt cries. "I took Batman last week. We get to bring something every year to share with the class—"

"Week. Every week," I correct him. Roxy throws side-eye in my direction.

"Tell me all about it, buddy, while your sister takes care of the mail." Roxy sits on the bottom step of the staircase, and Wyatt plops on the floor.

I leave the two of them and drop the envelope at Mom's place at the table, then my fear hits me all over again. I know what I need to tell Roxy, but what if she doesn't think I'm cool anymore?

Does it matter what she thinks? I ask myself.

"It kind of does," I whisper out loud.

Hands sweating, I'm more nervous now than I was at the Con six weeks ago.

"I wanted to tell you," I say to Roxy without looking at her. We're standing outside my closed bedroom door. I don't know why I'm freaking out so bad—I've already sent her the picture. "But I didn't want you to think it was lame."

I open the door, and there's all my stuff from the Realm. As worried as I am about how Roxy will react, a bigger part of me feels . . . happy . . . to see it like this. Like this is what it's *supposed* to look like.

"You brought all your old stuff back out," Roxy says. I'm still not looking at her, but her tone doesn't sound angry or mean. Just . . . matter-of-fact.

"I never wanted to put it away," I explain. "I really love this stuff."

"And you've been being weird because you wanted your old comforter back on your bed?"

Finally I turn to her. "It's not my bedroom, Roxy. It's me. I love this stuff still. Like, really love it. I entered a contest . . ." I trail off. She's watching me steadily, like she's waiting for what I'm going to say next. But it's the plain purple hoodie, the striped blue-and-white tee, and the black yoga pants that she's wearing that make me slow down. This is the uniform of the popular girls. This is what's in my closet. It's what I wear all the time. And none of it is *mine*. I don't belong. I've never belonged.

"And . . . ?" Roxy says. "You entered a contest and . . . ?"

"And I won," I say. "Then, at FanCon in Boston, I was on a panel about the Nightshade universe. And now I'm in another contest."

And the words come, and I tell her everything: about the challenges, talking with Hugh, about how I was kicking the boys' butt at the game . . . all of it.

She sits on my bed as I talk, tracing the mountain ranges on the map.

"So you hid it?" she says finally. "All of this?"

I nod. "I didn't want you, Jess D., and Hannah to think I was lame and stop talking to me. And I knew Tucker would hate it, which is fine because I don't want to go to the dance with him, anyway —"

Whoops. I hadn't necessarily meant for *that* to slip out.

Roxy shakes her head. "Sarah Anne, you've been *lying*. All this time! I don't care if you still like MK Nightshade or whatever. I care that you haven't told me the truth. In, like, *years*. We're supposed to be best friends."

"I know that. But I . . . You make fun of that stuff, about other people," I say. "So I thought you'd do the same to me." I trace the outline of the Wild Woods on my bed. That way I don't have to look at her.

Roxy sighs. "Fair. But if I'd known you were into it I wouldn't have made fun."

"Like you didn't make fun of Zoe? Or laugh when Jess D. tripped Nirmal?" I cock my eyebrow at her. I'm really good at that.

She sighs.

"The other stuff . . . just isn't me. I'm sorry, Roxy. I'm not cool. I'm more like Hugh than you."

Roxy doesn't say anything. And as we're sitting there, I think about all the lacrosse games we've played, all the time I've spent at her house or her at my house, all the silly conversations we've had . . . and I realize that things haven't been like that for a while. A long while.

Finally, Roxy turns to me. "I need to think about this. It's the lying, Sarah Anne, not just that you like this stuff. You pretended to be someone you aren't. Who are you?"

I pretended because I wanted us to stay friends, I think.

"An Adventurer of the Realm," I answer.

50

I meet Hugh outside the gym for the Science Showcase. We're not going to win—I think Nirmal and his perpetually sleeping partner are doing something with rockets, which will totally get first prize—but our data is good and our info slides look amazing, thanks to Hugh. So I'm pretty sure we'll get a good grade. I'm even hoping for an honorable mention or something.

Tonight Nightshade, Ink, will also announce the winner of the Fantastic Fan contest. So at some point I need to check my stats.

"Got everything?" Hugh asks. I nod. He's carrying a grocery bag with different types of potato chips and a box with our materials. I have the poster board and our raw data and notes to show the judges.

He nudges the door open and there's a rush of noise into the quiet of the hall. Tables are set up in rows, kids are putting out their projects, and parents and teachers stand in clumps or try to help. A big banner hangs from the ceiling reading SCIENCE SHOWCASE.

A parent volunteer gives us our table number, and we go down the rows until we find it. Our spot is sandwiched between a pair of kids who grew plants using different types of light and a group that measured the amount of sugar in sports drinks.

Coach Vaughn always tells us not to drink those things, even though the purple kind is my favorite. I make a mental note not to look at their results. And another one to keep Coach Vaughn away from their table.

Hugh shakes potato chips into bowls that are labeled with their flavors, and I set up our informational poster.

Mr. O'Malley comes around, checking on everyone's progress. He nods approvingly at our display and takes a sour cream 'n' cheddar chip out of one of our bowls.

"Do you have your memory stick?" he asks, munching.

Hugh digs through his pocket and hands it over. We had to make a couple of data slides that become part of a slideshow that runs during the night.

Mr. O'Malley checks us off on his clipboard and looks at our device. "Want to put your name on that?"

Hugh seems confused. "Sorry. I thought I did." He takes it back, grabs a Sharpie off our table, and prints his last name and student ID number on the blue plastic casing. Mr. O'Malley moves on to the plant group.

"I could've sworn I wrote my name on that thing," Hugh mutters.

I shrug. "Probably wiped off when it was in your bag. That happens all the time."

Hugh doesn't seem convinced, but whatever.

A few minutes later, we're ready. Now we just have to wait until the official start time of the Showcase. We decide to take turns walking around the gym, looking at the other projects. Someone is supposed to stay with our stuff at all times. And considering we have food at our table, we definitely can't leave our project alone.

Hugh leaves. I munch on a couple of chips and then remind myself to leave some for the Showcase attendees. I wipe up the crumbs, talk with the plant group, and wait.

Just as I'm starting to get bored, I spot Tucker. He and Jerry are wandering down the aisle in my direction, goofing at each of the tables. They stop at a group diagonally across from me, where the kids have done a project that involved making slime. They've made pyramids out of small plastic containers of ingredients. And clearly, obviously without caring, Tucker flicks a container right in the middle of one of the stacks, causing the top of that pyramid to collapse. He jumps back in mock innocence, hands in the air.

"Whoa! You didn't stack those very well," he says. He and Jerry double over laughing.

Meanwhile, one of the lids has popped off, splashing their poster. The ink smears. The kids are totally upset, and I'm mad.

Tucker and Jerry come to my table next.

"Sucks for them," Tucker says.

"That was a jerk move," I say. My hands shake a little.

"Did you fix that lacrosse situation?" he asks, ignoring my comment and taking a huge handful of chips from the bowl.

"Leave some for the rest of the world," I snap at him. I'm so done. It's funny, just a few days ago I didn't want to go to the dance with him, but keeping Roxy happy was the most important thing in the world.

And now—I am not going and I don't care if he knows it.

"I didn't even try to 'fix the situation,'" I say, mocking him. "I don't deserve to start. I've been slacking." Jerry, who had been busily stuffing chips in his face, pauses and stares at me, wide-eyed. I move the chip bowls off the table and out of reach. Hugh, back from his walk, comes up behind them.

"Not cool, Sarah Anne," Tucker says. He frowns at me. "You're my date."

"Not anymore," I say. I take a breath and gather my nerve. "I don't want to go with you because I think you're a jerk, and I don't hang around with jerks." I say the last part staring straight at Tucker. "Jess D. wants to go with you instead. Take her. You're a better fit."

I don't know what to expect, and neither does anyone else. Jerry and Hugh are frozen. My body is basically quivering with adrenaline and fear. Tucker looks at me like I'm not from Earth.

And then . . . he shrugs.

"Your loss." He stuffs his hands in his pockets and he and Jerry saunter away.

"Hey, Dork Boy," Tucker tosses at Hugh as they leave. "Have fun with Geek Girl over here. Lame."

Hugh steps closer to the table as they pass. "Uhhh . . ." he says. His cheeks are pink.

Geek Girl. I kind of like the sound of that.

51

The gym doors open, and parents, teachers, and kids pour in.

The Showcase has finally started. Adults and kids come to our table, and we burn (and eat) potato chips and show our data. The slime kids borrowed a hair dryer from the hot air balloon table and minimized poster damage.

Roxy comes by, and it feels like we're talking through glass.

"Looks good," she says to both of us. She even asks Hugh about our data design on the poster. Roxy is into graphic design and layouts, and Hugh tells her about some program he used to make our graphs look cool. When she leaves, I feel a little lighter.

"Excuse me, everyone." Mr. O'Malley's voice comes across the PA system. "Apologies for the technical difficulties, but we've figured everything out and we're going to start the slideshow. You'll see data sets and images from each project up on the screen. This is a great way to get an idea of the work that each of these students has put into their projects."

There's some applause, then the slideshow starts. I watch it until I see our slides go by — Hugh added some pictures of burning potato chips and the mess we made on his kitchen table the day we worked at his house — and then I go back to monitoring how many chips are being eaten versus burned.

I'm talking with Roxy's mom when there's a *whoop! whoop!* over the loudspeaker. Like everyone, we look around. On the screen, where the Science Showcase stuff is supposed to be, is a video.

"Who's the Fantastic Fan?" reads the title in MK Nightshade font.

First, there's a shot of the banner at FanCon, then the crowds.

"What the . . . ?" Hugh says.

And then there's the panel. I'm leaning into the microphone, frowning, as we hear "This question is for the girl in pink — the girl in pink — the girl in pink." With each repetition of "pink," it cuts to my face. And I never answer the question.

I tear my eyes away from the screen. Kids have whipped out their phones to shoot the scene in the gym. Parents seem confused. Even Mr. O'Malley is transfixed.

Horror grows through me like vines up a brick wall. I'm rooted in place. *Where did this come from? Who did this? What is going on?*

The video changes: There's my confused face at the lacrosse game, staring at the camera as I'm left in the dust, the team running down the field.

My whole body tingles from mortification.

There's my fall — clearly not watching where I'm going, eyes on the camera and whatever the boys are doing, flying through the air like the most awkward bird to ever take flight. It reverses, and I am jerked up from the grass, and then it goes forward again.

I feel that jerk in my own stomach.

The video changes again—images of me dressed as an ice dragon, but at the end of the day, when my horns droop and the makeup is smudged.

There's a clip from my final video: "In short, I want to be the Fantastic Fan."

Like everyone, I can't look away.

And then the leaderboard flashes onto the screen. My SAM avatar rolls around the screen like a bowling ball. Some video mastermind animated it.

Mastermind.

I turn, shaking and sweating, to Hugh.

"You wrote your name on *your* memory stick," I say.

He gapes at me. "You think . . . my *brother*?!"

I nod. Gulp. And then: "I'm going to puke."

52

I make it to one of the big garbage cans in the corner of the gym and hurl an assortment of flavored potato chips into it. My skin prickles and itches so badly that I want to peel it off and run away, leaving a shell of myself behind to deal with all this.

The video plays through my yurk-fest, but then someone mercifully shuts the whole thing down. Too bad it is too late. Everyone watched it.

Wiping my mouth with the back of my hand, I cross the gym, eyes on the floor, to get to a water fountain to rinse my mouth. My whole body trembles.

Why did he do this? What's the point, even?

But I have no answers. It's just cruel—the same kind of cruel that Tucker pulls all the time. No wonder I have such a bad taste in my mouth.

Now that the projector is off, the room gradually returns to normal. Parents and kids go back to checking out the projects, although the noise level is different. I'm guessing that most of the conversations are not about science.

I don't know where to go or what to do. Going back to the table doesn't seem like the right idea—I don't want to deal with everyone who comes by asking me about the freak-show video—but I literally have no place to go. My parents had to take Wyatt to an Explorer Scouts meeting and were coming here after.

I press my back against the gym wall, close my eyes, and wish to be invisible.

"Sarah Anne. Hey. Sarah Anne." Hannah. She nudges my arm. I don't open my eyes.

"Go away," I say. I cross my arms.

"Closing your eyes won't make me disappear," she says.

I crack open my eyes a tiny bit. She's wearing a green plaid skirt, white button-down shirt tied at the waist, and her silver-and-green necklace—looking every bit like she belongs at her table about how snakes move.

She leans against the wall next to me.

"Who did that?" she asks. She legit sounds concerned for me.

"Hugh's brother. I'm competing against him in this contest. . . ." Ugh. I don't want to go into this with anyone, let alone Hannah. "It doesn't matter. You wouldn't get it."

She frowns. "Why not?"

"Because you're you. You're not into that stuff. You think it's lame, like everyone else."

Hannah just stands there. I keep going. "I'm into a fandom. Most people don't get it."

"Look at me, Sarah Anne." I skate my eyes in her direction. "No. *Really* look at me."

She moves to stand in front of me, hands on her hips. "Well?"

"Uh, you look cute?" I try. What the . . . ? While the entire school is talking about me dressed in costume as an ice dragon, we're playing fashion police?

Hannah stomps her foot. "LOOK."

Green plaid skirt, white shirt . . . and then I see it: Just above the skirt's hem is a snake. You can barely spot it in the plaid, but it's there. The necklace she always wears is a snake with glittery green eye chips. Her ring—also a snake. And today she has on a green beaded bracelet.

"Wait—*what*?!"

Hannah looks at me, nods solemnly. "Always."

Mind. Blown.

53

"You got this," she says. She's pumping me up like I'm a prize fighter in the corner of the ring. "You're fine. Hold on."

She disappears, then returns.

She hands me a cup of the purple sports drink, and I sip it gratefully. "You okay?" she says. La-la-la, Sugar Project Table.

"Yeah, I think so." I don't feel like puking anymore, and although I'm still shaky, even that is getting better.

"Good, 'cause O'Malley is looking for you."

Ugh.

Hannah stands next to me, escorting me through the gym.

"So that's what you were doing that day in the mall," Hannah says as we head back to the table. Her chatter is there to distract me from the puzzled looks people give us as we go by, and I'm thankful. "I took my picture with you!"

"Yeah, but I looked way better at the beginning of the day."

"Let me guess—Penny did your makeup?" I grin in response. "She's going to win an Oscar someday," Hannah finishes.

We're in our aisle, and Mr. O'Malley, Hugh, and my parents hover around our table. They all wear mixed expressions of concern and annoyance. Mom and Dad fuss over me. I cringe.

"Sorry," I say.

"Where were you?" Mr. O'Malley asks.

"Uh, I didn't feel so good," I reply. I guess I look pretty bad, because he doesn't respond.

"Told you," Hugh says.

"Hugh said that he thinks his brother did something to your presentation?" Mom asks.

I nod. "I've been competing against him in the contest, and he seems . . . upset . . . that I'm doing so well. I guess he wanted to embarrass me."

"And it worked," Hannah adds helpfully.

I glare at her.

"Is your brother here tonight?" my dad asks Hugh.

"I don't think he's coming," Hugh says. "But I know he's home. He's been using me too," Hugh adds. "He tricked me into answering all the questions to get him in in the first place, and I've been helping him ever since. He promised me he'd take me to the premiere if he won. And then I really didn't want to lose, at least until I realized that I was being a jerk about the whole thing too. I'm sorry, Sarah Anne." He flushes.

So *that's* why he got his brother's T-shirt, and put the balloons in my locker.

"Can you get him here?" I ask, suddenly getting an idea.

"Maybe?" Hugh says. "What do you have in mind?"

I turn to Mr. O'Malley. "Can I use your projector? Just at the end of the night?"

Mr. O'Malley runs his hands through his hair. "I can't show the slideshow anymore because the video will keep playing. So . . . sure? Just don't do anything that's going to get me into trouble."

"Never," I say.

Hugh whips out his phone, taps away, and shows me his text: Our flash drive got stepped on and crushed. Can you bring a copy of the slideshow down here?

Nice.

My parents, satisfied that I'm not going to fall to pieces and not at all interested in being around for what I'm cooking up, decide to walk around and look at the other exhibits. Mr. O'Malley shakes his head and leaves with them.

Roxy, Jess D., Tucker, and Jerry come over as soon as they're gone. They were waiting.

"You must be *so* embarrassed," Jess D. coos.

"I'm over it," I say. "It's easier now that everyone knows the truth." I direct this to Roxy, whose face is closed off to me.

"I hope you weren't going to wear that dragon outfit to the dance," Tucker says. I cock my head at him.

"Really?" I snap.

"Let's go," Roxy says. "You coming?" she asks Hannah.

Everyone turns to her. She looks from me, to Jess D., to Roxy, Tucker, and Jerry.

"I'm staying," she says.

As they leave, I see Jess D. smiling.

She's getting what she wants. For a minute, anger flares through me. But what it leaves behind is sadness. It's over with Roxy, for sure. What's left of that friendship is done. Hannah comes to my side.

"Their loss," she says. I smile at her, grateful that she and Hugh can forgive my lies.

Time to move forward. I draw Hannah and Hugh around the table. "Okay, here's what we're going to do. . . ."

54

The Showcase is going to end soon, and Chris hasn't shown up yet. Hugh has texted him two more times, telling him that we really need that flash drive, but . . . nothing.

And then I spot him.

"Here he comes," I whisper to Hugh, even though I don't have to whisper because Chris is at the end of our row and it's still loud in here. But whispering is dramatic.

I try to make my face go normal, not like the total freak-out that I feel inside.

He approaches the table.

"Here's your flash drive, dork. Take better care of your stuff," Chris says snidely. He sneers at me.

"Think you're going to win tonight, Sam?"

I shrug. "Probably."

Hugh disappears with the flash drive. Chris steps away from the table. If he messed with the slideshow again, he doesn't want to be around when it plays.

I need to keep him here.

"The results come in at nine, right?" I call. Chris turns.

"Yeah," he says. "Pretty soon."

"I turned my video in so late," I say, stalling. *What's Hugh doing? Hurry up!*

Chris shrugs. "Too bad for you," he says.

"Bad for you too. I mean, there's no way you're going to win, regardless of what happens to me."

Chris puffs up a little, like an angry penguin.

"I might."

"Nah," I say.

Just then, the familiar *whoop! whoop!* rings through the gym. Everyone stops to look at the screen. Up on the wall, super huge and in big block letters, there's a new slideshow. It reads:

CHRIS THOUGHT HE WAS AN MK NIGHTSHADE FANTASTIC FAN.

BUT HE'S BEEN USING HIS BROTHER'S KNOWLEDGE FOR THE WHOLE CONTEST.

AND SABOTAGING THE OTHER CONTESTANTS!

Photo of them unfurling the banner at the lacrosse game . . . photo of the awful slideshow . . .

BECAUSE HE DOESN'T WANT TO GET BEATEN BY A GIRL.

Photo of me in full ice dragon makeup in our kitchen (before it got melty and weird).

Photo of me at our science table.

The slideshow starts over, and I feel relief. It's done. Everyone knows the whole story, knows who I am, this time on my terms. Hugh really did an impressive job with it in such a short amount of time.

Chris stands rooted to the gym floor like someone planted him there. His face is waxy pale. There's a low rumble from the remaining parents, and the kids at the Showcase hoot and catcall. Who knows how many of them knew about the contest before, but they all know now.

"That's so . . . so . . . bogus!" Chris yells, finally finding his voice.

"'Bogus'? Really?" Hannah says. "That's all you've got?"

He heads toward the door.

"I've already sent a copy of this to Nightshade, Ink!" I call after him. He raises a finger behind his back in response.

Hugh comes back to the table with the flash drive. The slideshow is off.

"How'd it go? I couldn't see it from the projector."

I laugh. "He didn't take it well."

Hugh grins. "I'm sure he'll kill me later, but it was worth it."

Hannah steps in. "Hey—we should check and see who won, right? I mean, you need to think about your outfit for the premiere!"

257

I shrug. "If you want. I don't really care anymore," I say. And I'm surprised to find that I actually really don't.

Hugh and Hannah lean over Hannah's phone, looking it up. I step away from them.

I've come back to myself, or started to. This is the beginning of who I really am.

"We've got the results!" Hannah says.

Well, maybe I care a little.

I step forward to see.

A COUPLE OF WEEKS LATER

Nirmal takes the basketball-sized tub of popcorn from my hands.

"Watch this," he says, and pours it into one of the cardboard boxes that you use if you're carrying multiple snacks and sodas to your seat.

"What are you doing?" Holly Yee asks.

"I'm a rewards member. I get a free refill!" He takes the empty popcorn bucket and returns to the concession line. I'm left holding a mountain of delicious-smelling buttery goodness. I make sure that none of it gets on my Lady Althena hoodie.

"Sarah Anne! Hey!" I turn, and Hugh and the rest of the Fandom Club have gathered around the giant Sir Oakheart cutout advertising *A Glut of Ghosts*. It's the official release night, and this is our first club outing.

Holly and I join the group. Everyone's posed around the knight: Hannah; Hugh; Eloise and her friend; Callan and Jake, two seventh-grade *Star Wars* fans; and some of the gamer kids. Nirmal holds his second giant popcorn with one arm and whips out his phone to take our picture.

Behind Nirmal, Roxy, Jerry, Tucker, and Jess D. cross the movie theater lobby. The girls trail the boys, giggling and whispering to each other. Jess D. sees me and scowls, linking her arm through Roxy's, as though I'm going to swoop in and take her away. Not a chance.

"Are you ever going to stop wearing that?" Hugh says. I take my eyes off the girls. Hugh's pointing to my Nightshade Hollywood premiere lanyard.

"Probably never," I say with a grin. Nirmal tries to get our attention, and a passing moviegoer takes Nirmal's phone so he can get in the shot. Somehow, I end up in the center of the whole group.

"Smile," our photographer says.

I do.

THE END

RULES FOR BLENDING IN, NOT GEEKING OUT:

1. ~~KEEP YOUR GEEK ON THE DOWN LOW.~~
A "Fantastic Fan" panel at a con?
NOT down low. Just not.

2. ~~GEEK-OUTS LEAD TO FREAK-OUTS.~~
Does the Science Showcase debacle count?
Yeah. Yeah, it does.

3. ~~DON'T WEAR YOUR GEEK ON YOUR SLEEVE.... OR~~
~~BAG. OR PANTS. OR SOCKS.~~
Or on your face. As an ice dragon. *headdesk*

4. ~~KEEP YOUR GEEK ONLINE.~~
Like some night when you answer over one
hundred questions for some silly contest?

5. ~~DON'T TALK GEEK FOR LONG.~~
Especially in the kitchen of your biggest
competitor's brother.

6. ~~ALL ROADS LEAD TO YOUR GEEK,~~
~~BUT DON'T GO DOWN THEM.~~
Too late.

7. ~~GEEK POSTERS ARE NOT DECOR.~~
~~KEEP THEM OFF YOUR WALLS.~~
Until you realize that being surrounded by
what you love gives you strength.

ACKNOWLEDGMENTS

Publishing a book requires a whole team, and I would not be able to do it without the wonderful people on mine:

Sally Harding, my agent, who believes in my stories and encourages me through every step of the process.

Erin Black, my editor, whose insight, thoughtful feedback, and enthusiasm for this book brought Sarah Anne's story to life.

The Scholastic team, including Josh Berlowitz and Kerianne Okie (who fix my mistakes and find inconsistencies. Anything left is mine), Jordana Kulak in publicity (who promotes the book), and Maeve Norton, who designed the cover and interiors (making the book look amazing!).

My critique group: Gary Crespo, Wendy McDonald, Megan Mullin, Phoebe Sinclair, and Annette Trossello, who read multiple drafts with patience, insight, and high standards.

My writing buddy, Nancy Werlin, who keeps me on task, helps me solve plot problems, and giggles with me over the funny stuff.

Will O'Malley, friend and science teacher extraordinaire, and Grace O'Malley, who taught me to play lacrosse.

My friend Pam Vaughan, who coaches, supports, and cheers me on.

The Montserrat College of Art students who educated me on rules of their fandoms, cosplay, and LARPing.

The Writers' Loft, which provides me not only a wonderful space in which to write but also a community to support this work.

The Mildest Women: Toni Buzzeo, Jackie Davies, Loree Griffin Burns, Kim Harrington, Joan Paquette, Diana Renn, and Nancy Werlin, who lift me up and set me on the right path over and over again.

Charlotte and Harker, my children, who I love like crazy.

And Frank, the best husband, partner, and *Star Wars* geek a girl could ask for.